NOT HOME FOR THE Holidays

ISABELLE DRAKE

For more information contact:
Riverdale Avenue Books
5676 Riverdale Avenue
Riverdale, NY 10471
www.riverdaleavebooks.com

Design by www.formatting4U.com
Cover by Scott Carpenter

Digital ISBN: 978162601
Print ISBN: 9781626016675

First Edition, December 2019
Second Edition, November 2023

Dedication

For my daughters.
Brillant, brave, and beautiful.

Dear Gentle Reader,

No doubt you have noticed that Not Home for the Holidays is inspired by the always popular Hallmark Christmas films. If you've watched a couple of these, you know the story is often focused on an overworked woman who has lost touch with her family and friends. She has lost touch with the importance of holidays such as Thanksgiving, Christmas, and all the others which might be a Hallmark card occasion. We meet our harried heroine two weeks before Christmas as she reluctantly returns to her quaint, snowy, small hometown. She runs smack into a handsome, bearded guy wearing a beautifully soft flannel shirt. The guy is holding the hand of an adorable toddler, or he is looking as though he ought to be holding the hand of an adorable toddler. Or perhaps he is looking as though he will soon be looking as though he ought to be holding the hand of an adorable toddler.

The moment is awkward for her. How could it not be? The poor woman has completely lost touch with humanity. It's much less awkward for him. He, after all, is not only in touch with humanity, but he is also calm, kind, friendly, and reassuring. These are key qualities to have when one is in the midst of a meet cute. The moment passes, and the two of them go their separate ways... until, surprise, it turns out that they are working together to save an historic bed and breakfast, bookstore, hat shop, or goat farm.

Obviously, because they are working together during the holiday season, they fall in love. He saves her from herself, and she… well… she does something practical like a thorough forensic accounting of the struggling business and by doing so saves the place in peril. Once the saving is complete, they declare that their love will last forever.

She gives up her high stress life. They move into the historic home at the goat farm and decide to renovate everything within a five-mile radius so that they can turn the place into an Airbnb tailored to bookstore owners who like to do baby goat yoga. As the credits roll, we know what their future holds. He will find the hand of a toddler (perhaps their own) to hold; she will continue to work hard doing all the practical things that need doing. She must. Running an historic farm that caters to bookstore owners who enjoy baby goat yoga is, frankly, quite a lot of work. Most importantly, though, they will live a happy, Instagram story-worthy life together. Ahhh. Bliss.

If you've read my other work, you know I love romance and romance stories. I've written sweet, sexy, and erotic romances. I've written short, long, series, and standalone stories. Prior to creating Emma and Ethan's story, the one type I had not yet written was the holiday romance.

The inspiration for and the invitation to write a Hallmark Christmas in reverse story came to me one spring afternoon while I was seated in a row of black vinyl chairs and half-watching Pimp My Ride. Beyond the huge single-pane window at the end of the row of chairs was a stunning view of the interior of a garage. The whirr of air compressors and hum of car engines rumbled through the glass, punctuated occasionally by a shout. To my left and to my right were others doing exactly what I was doing: scrolling through their phones, half watching the ever-cool guys at West Coast Customs transform what I think was a late 80's Cadillac Eldorado. My scrolling was on Twitter; I was reading the same thread that pops up occasionally, a conversation about the predictability of Hallmark Christmas films. This time the conversation had a twist: what if someone wrote a Hallmark Christmas in reverse. Lori Perkins, the publisher of Riverdale Avenue Books, posted that she'd love to see such a book. I posted that I'd love to write it.

And there it was, the challenge. My curiosity sparked, I started to imagine what elements I'd flip and which ones I'd keep. Obviously, the meet cute and happy ending would stay. The sparkling, festive, snowy backdrop as well as the all-over feel good vibe, also were a must. For the flip, I focused on the heroine. I wanted to move her from a rural location to an urban one and take her from a sort-of successful career into a high pressure very successful one. The hero, I also wanted to flip. Why not a man seeking to get out of his high stress job?

I knew I wanted the happy ending for my story to be a small-town girl accepting a high-pressure job and moving to a city to be with a business-suit-wearing urbanite. Inspired by my personal favorite Christmas movies, I selected New York for my city. Inspired by my own experiences with country living, I added in some chickens and small-town drama.

Holiday cheers,
Isabelle Drake, 2023

Dear Santa,

As you know, this past year has been a rough one.

If I ask you for an extra special Christmas this year, you might start imagining glittering snow, cozy family gatherings, sweet-faced children making cookies, and feisty senior citizens getting into everyone else's business. You might start thinking I want a holiday season like one of those Christmas romance movies featuring a crazed workaholic woman who needs to learn how to slow down and appreciate life and set aside her own dreams and replace them with someone else's. That someone else being a steady small-town man who knows the value of family.

You know I live in that small town, like the ones in the movies. There are barns and cozy houses, there are generations of traditions, there are football games and parades, and yes, there are many sturdy small-town guys who know about animals and can work with their hands and have loads of country charm. I even had that flannel-shirted, small-town guy. Had. Past tense.

The point is, I'd like a different sort of holiday romance. I'm not the sort of person to give up on my dreams just because some handsome guy tells me I should slow down and appreciate the little things. Like if I do, then he'll find me worthy. And I'm not the kind of girl who fits into that stereotypical, small-town, feel good about giving up on a successful career so you can start an apron collection scene.

If you're cool with all of that, I'm open for what you have stashed in your bag.

If not, well, I guess it's the naughty list for me.

With hope and thanks,
Emma

Chapter One

It's the middle of December, first thing in the morning, in southern Michigan. Fat snowflakes are skittering through the dawn sky, and the winter air is country crisp and angel quiet. My dad's cow barn, off in the distance, has a stream of smoke coming up from his wood burning stove. The roof is capped with heavy white snow, glowing from the last rays of the moon. Outside is picture perfect.

I'm not outside.

I'm in my chicken coop, trying to get ready to go live on Insta like I do every Wednesday at sunrise. My feed is for my business, City Chicks, so I need the setting inside to be picture perfect too. But the birds are not cooperating. Instead of sitting nicely in their cute-as-can-be tin nesting boxes, cooing and being adorable, they've all tumbled out and are clucking and fluttering, racing in tight circles around my legs.

Something is wrong, they want me to know. *Something isn't right!*

As far as I'm concerned, the only thing that's wrong is that they aren't looking charming or fresh or video ready. After spending 10 minutes trying to get ready to go live, neither am I. It's stuffy in the coop. I'm getting sweaty, my messy bun is becoming too messy, and the selfie stick has chosen today to finally and truly fall apart.

My phone is on the floor of the coop, covered in cedar shavings. This is my big last-minute holiday shopping push. Only about two weeks until Christmas. I need this live feed to go and go well.

The sun came over the snow-covered fields 25 minutes ago, putting me about 18 minutes later than I started last week. I need to get this mess together and do a proper hello like I've done every mid-week morning for the past six months. That's when I started taking pics of my hens.

The posts caught on.

Now I'm *that* chicken girl, one of the quaint country folks posting idyllic rural pics. My twist—I'm showing off the girls in all their glory to sell feed and chicken-raising supplies from my Amazon store. I'm not the bragging type, but since it's just you and me, I can say that business is good. Since I added my YouTube channel, it's been really good, actually.

Ugh. Now Louisa, the one hen I can usually depend on to look darling, is fighting with Cluck Norris, the bantam rooster.

A couple weeks ago, I bought him just for show, you know, to give the coop some color and sassiness. He's a beautiful rusty Red Cochin. Really pretty. Unfortunately, as of this morning, he's decided he's the boss of everything and has taken to antagonizing the hens. Typical guy. He's feathered up and crowing like a madman, hopping across the floor. His feet skitter over my phone. Yuck. Next thing I know, he's in the far corner by the tiny door that leads outside and into the yard. Louisa, crouched down and steady gazed, is planning her next attack. I swipe the sweat off the sides of my face as I kick open the small hatch door, shoo him out, then shut it.

One problem solved.

Now, time to get this show started.

"Hey babe."

I hear his words off in the distance but don't turn around.

I stare down at the busted selfie stick. Did the dark side of my mind conjure him up?

The door behind me squeaks open and the floor vibrates from his footsteps. He makes another sound, this one never turning into words. "Ummm…"

The sweaty chill on my skin turns to bitter cold as I continue wrestling with the selfie stick, pretending the little piece of plastic that holds the phone in place isn't completely broken off. I feel him coming up behind me, smell him, and I stiffen. Not from fear. From pain.

He's behind me now. "Give it here. Let me see if I can fix it."

He says it so naturally, like we're still a couple. Like him stopping by and appearing in my life spontaneously is still a normal, pleasant and welcome event. Childish, I know, to think I can wish him and the dread he's brought with him away, but there I am doing exactly that.

He tells me that he likes my dress, and I cringe.

It's a bright red sweater dress I paired with hunter green muck boots. To capture that holiday vibe. But without the selfie stick the boots won't show in the picture. Maybe if I get down on the floor, swing my calves toward my thighs, and hold the phone up high, I'll be able to get the boots in. If I sit on the ground, the shavings will stick to the wool. But the last time I showed off these boots I sold eight pairs in three hours.

He taps my shoulder, asks again to see the selfie stick which I'm now clinging to as though it can save me from the searing humiliation churning through me like toxic waste. I don't turn to look into his green eyes. I continue to pretend he isn't there, longing for him to vanish, fade into some abyss. Or at least back into his shiny black F150 which is probably parked out in front of the century-old farmhouse where I live with my dad.

Accepting his offer of help or asking him to hold the phone for me is out of the question. So, I disregard him, continue to pretend he isn't there. I start carefully lowering myself into the mess of shavings awaiting me on the floor of the coop. My phone buzzes. I miss the notification. Whatever it is, it'll have to wait until later.

While I was ignoring him, he'd continued talking behind me, asking me over and over if I'm going to talk to him. At this point I have two choices. Talk to him and delay my live feed, or go live with him in the background, loitering there, distracting me, and making me feel like crap all over again.

From my spot in the midst of the chicken shavings, I pivot and glare into the eyes that used to make me quiver in a completely different way. "What do you want?"

The hens are still making noise, only now it's more of a frenzy. This is partly because I'm sitting on the floor. Chickens don't like it when people do things out of the ordinary. No matter the cause, I'm actually kind of thankful for their hysteria because their cackling provides a distraction and, as a bonus, make it hard to carry on a conversation.

He's frowning. "Why do you have to be so hostile, Emma?"

I'm not going to say the reason aloud. Not then, not ever again. I repeat my question, letting the hostility ooze. "What do you want?"

"I didn't know it was going to be like this. I thought you'd... you'd..."

"Not be mad anymore? I'm not mad." I say the words like they make me sick because they do. The word *mad* doesn't even come close to capturing how I feel which is mostly stupid for believing he cared about me and that we had a future together.

"I want to tell you something," he says, taking a step back.

"Another lie?" I pause, catch my nerve, then continue. "It's been almost a month since I've heard one from you. So please. Go ahead."

Louisa runs across his boot. Two of the other hens flutter up to the roosting bar, their pale orange feet gripping the wood tightly as they peer over at the two of us. He stares at them for a few seconds, then turns to me. "I have to ask you something. A favor."

My chest tightens and the tension drops down deep into my body. For the first time, I'm glad I'm sitting down. "Please, go ahead."

He shrugs, about what I don't know, then says, "They moved Granna to hospice. About a week ago."

Sad but not surprised, I nod. His grandmother has been fighting cancer for a couple years. Despite how I feel about him, I'm sad about the news.

"Would you..." he trails off and looks toward the windows that run alongside the back of the coop as he runs one hand through his dark red hair. Wavy hair that I myself ran my fingers through on many, many occasions.

The sun is officially up now, and the rooster is letting us all know. His crow is shrill and sharp, cutting through the silence at odd intervals.

When there is a break in the noise, he turns to me,

7

connects his eyes with mine, then asks, "Will you come with me to visit her?"

"Have you already been to see her?"

Both his hands are at his side now. "Yeah."

"Then why do you need me?" But that's about him, not about her. I don't need him to go see her. I could just go… but last time we 'talked' he fessed up to the fact that he still hadn't told Granna 'we'd' broken up.

It's his turn to stay quiet, sliding his hands into the pockets of his jeans as he looks around. The hens have settled down. Now, it's mostly quiet in the coop, except for the rooster, less excited about the sun and now annoyed about being kicked out. He's stopped crowing, but I can hear him pecking at the wood, furious and frustrated. I can relate.

"Will ya, Emma? Come with me?"

Oh, great. Now he's trying to use his country charm. Too late, I'm immune now. I've been totally immunized. For life.

The minutes are ticking by. I've already lost both the warm tones of the sunrise and my enthusiasm for the session. Soon I'll have also lost my enthusiasm for my business, the chickens, and making it through the day.

Granna is losing more than that.

He's waiting by the door of the coop. I'm going to say yes, and we both know it. I set my wrists on my knees and tap the Insta app. The feed pops. "What day? When?"

"Friday? If we get there at 11:00, we can eat lunch with her."

I nod without looking at him.

"Pick you up at 10:30?"

Staring at my phone, I nod again.

"Hey, Emma? I'm sorry. You didn't deserve that, what I did."

This time I don't nod. I just keep staring at my screen until I hear the door click shut.

After a couple deep breaths, I shake away the visible signs of my distress, pull what I hope will be a happy expression onto my face, adjust the phone so both my boots and dress are visible hit live, then start talking.

* * *

Once I'm done in the chicken coop, I find my dad in his office at the front of the cow barn. The space is cozy from the wood burner. It also smells like cow shit. Add in hay, dirt and diesel gas and that's the scent of my childhood. My dad is seated at his computer, looking like he's reading email. In his plaid flannel shirt, brown Dickies work pants and Tigers baseball cap he looks exactly the same as he does every day of my life. His steadiness is a comfort I really should appreciate more. I drop myself into the battered wood chair next to his desk. My father is Deaf, so I wait until he looks up to say hello.

When he turns to me, I spot a smudge of dirt above his dark eyebrow, his deep brown eyes already tired. I sign "hi," then use my hands to tell him I'm done with the sunrise Insta feed. After he gives me a thumbs up, he uses his hands to ask me what's wrong. I'm not surprised he sees the distress on my face. Ever since my mom passed away 10 months ago, we're closer than ever. No secrets here. I tell him about the surprise visit and how I agreed to go see Granna tomorrow.

My dad frowns but his fingers stay on the edge of the desk. I shrug, trying to let him know it isn't a big deal. Knowing it is, he shakes his head, then asks about my plans for the day. I fill him in on the little stuff, kiss him on the cheek, sign "bye," then stand to leave. As I step away from the desk, an envelope catches my eye. It's a large brown one, with a handwritten address. It's been opened, then resealed. My dad sees me looking at it, and something passes between us. My heart tightens. I wait. He offers no explanation, so I turn and walk out.

Chapter Two

"Uncle E? Do you think this is enough sprinkles?"

Ethan stopped scrolling through his email to look over the top edge of his laptop. "Sure. It looks great."

An annoyed scoff was followed by a complaint. "You didn't even look. You have to thoroughly assess the situation before offering a judgment."

Ethan lowered his computer screen and inspected the scene across from him on his kitchen countertop. His nephew Carlson was pressing red and green sprinkles, alternately and one at a time, into the white frosting covering a Christmas tree shaped sugar cookie. The nine-year-old was applying the decorations with the diligence of a Freshman engineering student engrossed in chemistry lab.

"It seems you have the surface sufficiently covered," he said after a moment.

"What about the trunk?" Carlson pointed to the tiny bit at the bottom, the only remaining space where the white was visible.

"Are trunks usually green or red?"

"No." The boy scoffed again. "They're brown."

"Then you have your answer."

"Indeed, I do." Carlson swept that cookie, now complete, aside then slid another into his workstation. *Rudolph the Red-Nosed Reindeer* came up in their

11

playlist, and he began singing along as he approached the cookie with the same intensity.

Ethan raised his screen, then went back to searching for the email containing the details on his marketing and advertising agency's contest, Media Matters. He'd been looking for the message for almost 10 minutes. Why hadn't he paid more attention to it? Why hadn't he printed it out and secured it in a folder? So what if he thought social media was a waste of time. Not something to be taken seriously by business marketers. Who spends valuable time clicking through random pictures posted by people they don't know? People they'll never know.

Regardless of his opinion, he had agreed to be present next week when the contest finalists were interviewed and evaluated. That round of meetings would be one of his final obligations with the agency.

"Uncle E?"

Ethan straightened and looked over the top edge of the screen. Carlson had dumped out a pile of sprinkles. Using a table knife and the precision of a pharmacist, he was organizing decorations into separate piles of red and green.

"Um, mmm?" Ethan glanced back down, started scrolling through his email again.

"Mom says you're giving up and quitting."

Leave it to his oldest sister to put her nose into his business. "I am not giving up."

He lowered the screen again. With the organization completed, the application of the sprinkles went much more quickly. Soon, Carlson was halfway through coating the cookie in front of him. Red sprinkle. Green sprinkle. Red sprinkle.

"I'm refocusing my priorities," Ethan said, making

a mental note to tell Beatrice to keep her concerns to herself. "And, since you are one to appreciate accuracy, I'm not quitting. I'm becoming a silent partner."

"You aren't going to talk?"

"That's right. I have people to talk for me. Highly qualified people." People who knew better what to say and do.

Eyes focused down, the boy nodded. "I can appreciate that."

At least someone was on his side. If only he could get Carlson to convince his mother and then Ethan's three other siblings. "Thank you."

"Aside from not talking, what are you new priorities?"

Good question. He probably should have an answer to that, but the truth of the matter was that he did not. All he was certain of was that he'd lost his passion for his work, and that if he stayed in his position the agency would suffer. The small but mighty agency his parents created had been around for decades. The idea of it falling apart now, because of him, was frankly too terrible to consider. If only there was a quick fix for lack of enthusiasm and creative talent. He'd tried though. Tried everything he could think of to get excited about his position at the top. To recreate himself into someone hipper and more modern. Alas, he was a pinstriped, suspender-wearing, shoe shining, traditional sort of guy. The kind of guy who never colored outside the lines and who always put his crayons back exactly in the spot they'd originally come from.

Carlson looked up, his face expectant. "How about a girlfriend? Mom says you've been alone too long. She says you need a woman."

Ethan managed to hold in his sigh. That wasn't a new comment. "Your mom has a lot to say."

He nodded again. "It's true. She does."

Ethan took a sip of his hot cocoa, then set the mug down with a light thump. "Do *you* have a girlfriend?"

After rolling his eyes, his nephew replied. "Did you have a girlfriend when you were nine?"

"As you were kind enough to point out, I don't even have one now." He held his breath. When was the last time he'd even been on a date? Last summer? He'd taken someone to a wedding… a woman he'd gone to grad school with. Nancy? Nellie? Norma? The sigh finally slipped out.

Carlson put the last sprinkle on the cookie then offered it to Ethan. "Want a cookie?"

The thing was nearly dripping with frosting and probably had twice as many calories as it should due to the sprinkles. Careful to take it by the edges, he accepted it. "Is my single state so pathetic that you feel the need to pacify me with sweets?" He made a point of looking at the mug of cocoa his nephew had insisted he drink.

"It works for me when I'm sad." Carlson placed another frosted cookie in front of him and began the sprinkle application process again. Red sprinkle. Green sprinkle.

Who said he was sad? He wasn't sad. Or lonely. He was simply taking control of his life.

Using his free hand, Ethan began scrolling, looking for that email. Finally, he spotted it with the subject line: Christmas promo event. He took a bite of the cookie, crunched on the sprinkles as he read through the message. Five finalists, five presentations, five interviews, and some contest challenges. All next week.

Then he was done.

Fine. He'd get through this last task, turn the

responsibilities over to his key staff, then go, as his mother was so fond of saying, 'find himself.'.

* * *

Friday, I'm dressed and waiting on the front porch of my house. It's only 10 after 11:00, so I have 20 full minutes of sitting or standing, waiting and dreading.

I pull out my phone, stare at it as though it can remind me of what has been niggling at the back of my memory ever since I woke up. There is something I was supposed to do, but I can't remember what it is. Lamely, I scroll through my Insta feed. Lots of likes and comments. Especially on the series of pics I took yesterday afternoon when the girls were scratching in the snow, looking country cute as they pecked at who knows what. I check my Amazon store for orders or messages, find nothing new or unresolved, then put my phone away. I hitch my bag higher up onto my shoulder and step off the porch, heading toward the cow barn. The gravel crunches under my boots, the same green ones from yesterday.

I step into the barn, glance around. Empty. No cows. No dad.

The office is also empty. I move toward the desk, scan the surface. There are some local newspapers and three coffee cups from the gas station in town. I take a few steps closer. I see a brown corner sticking out between an untidy pile of catalogs and flyers. I poke it with the tip of my finger. Whatever it is, it's not my business. I should trust my dad to tell me if it's something I need to know. Listening for the sound of footfalls, I poke it again, harder. It doesn't budge. I let out a deep breath, then start to lift the top half of catalogs and flyers, slowly, to keep the shape of the mess intact. In the distance, I hear a truck pulling into the driveway. Leave it to him to be early. I drop the stuff back in to place, remind myself to stand up straight, then head outside.

He's pulled up to the front porch, so I cross behind then tap on the window. He unlocks the door. I get in.

"Heya."

The scent of his soap is achingly familiar. I wish I didn't have to breathe.

"I don't have anything to say to you. Let's just go." I hold back the *please* and *if you don't mind*.

He nods. I clip on my seatbelt, hold my bag in my lap. About 30 minutes later, I'm walking to the front of the hospice building. He's beside me, not talking, not touching.

He stops me just outside the door. "Thanks again for coming."

"I didn't come for you," I reply, my gaze fixed on the wreath hanging on the door.

"I know." He tries to touch me. When I back away, he adds, "I can still say thanks."

"Yeah, you can. But I don't want you to." I step closer to the door, and it whooshes open. I go in and stand by a cluster of potted poinsettias as he checks in at the reception desk.

A few minutes later we're seated in the sunny front room. Under the bay window that faces the parking lot there's a puzzle, the pieces spread across a long narrow table. There are some random plants in mismatched pots and an aquarium. The hum of the filter, pumping air bubbles into the tank, is the only sound.

Granna comes in, walking slowly but her eyes bright and a smile on her mouth. My anxiety about being so near

16

to him softens, and I'm up on my feet, accepting her shaky hug.

"Beautiful as always, Emma. You are a welcome sight." She takes in my wool floral jacket and jeans. "Those boots add just the right amount of sass, don't they?"

I kiss her cheek, then step back, so she can hug him. Once the hellos are complete, she takes my hand but speaks to him, asking him directly if he agrees about the sassiness of the boots.

"I—I… Sure."

Her fingers are cool and fragile as she tugs me forward. "Come on," she says, nearly losing her grip on my hand. I gently glide my fingers out of her palm, them loop our arms. She grins, then looks ahead. "Down this way."

We must be part of the early lunch shift because the cafeteria is only about a third full. Most of the cozy round tables are empty and the ones that have people seated at them hold couples or groups of three. "Usually I eat in my room, but I made these special arrangements for today." After we sit, she adds, "I've already ordered our meal. I hope you like chicken." Seconds later, she's laughing softly. "I mean for eating, in this case, of course."

He looks lost, but laughter is spilling out of me, pulling more of the tension from my body. Granna and I are chuckling together now, setting our napkins in our laps and then she's on to some gossip about the other residents.

It isn't until dessert that she catches me off guard.

"I've been waiting this whole time but didn't want to ask. I can't wait any more. You must have heard by now." She sets her hands on the edge of the table. "Are you one of the finalists?"

I lower the spoonful of cherry Jell-O I'd just been about to slip into my mouth. The little square jiggles. It's her memory, I know.

She leans forward.

"I—I—" don't know what she's referring to. No point in explaining to her that she's gotten me confused with someone else. "No, I haven't heard yet."

Frowning, she pulls a small spiral-topped notebook from the floral tote bag beside her. The notebook is followed by a calendar. She opens the notebook, flips through the pages filled with notes, then opens the calendar and points to today's date. Tapping on the square representing yesterday, she says, "You should have heard Wednesday."

He's starting to look uncomfortable, and his mouth is opening and closing. "I—I was supposcd to tell you something."

I lift my eyebrows.

She closes the calendar, then tucks it back into the tote. "Oh, Emma, I knew I should have told you myself." She frowns at him. The expression isn't harsh as much as it's resigned. "How are you going to support her dreams if you don't remember these sorts of things?" She slides the little notebook over, and I start to read.

As I'm taking in her description of a small business contest, that niggling sensation starts again in the back of my mind. I take in more of the description, a contest searching for new small businesses that use social media in unique and inspiring ways. There is a promise of investment in the one chosen as winner from the pool of five finalists. There's nothing familiar about any of what's on the page, yet while I read it, I keep thinking there's something I've forgotten to do. While I'm reading, he's

18

talking to me, explaining all the reasons why he forgot to tell me about how Granna had asked him to tell me that she'd entered me in this contest.

Then it hits me—the email. I set down the tiny notebook and dig through my own bag for my phone. I open my non-junk mail email, and there it is. The message I'd received Wednesday morning while fighting with the selfie stick. I tap it open and scan through.

I'm a finalist.

I'm a finalist?

I set my phone down and touch Granna's arm. "I'm a finalist!"

"Of course you are, dear. I never doubted you would be."

"Excuse me, just a sec." I grab my phone again and read through the email. The information blurs together. I feel myself getting excited—someone picked my business City Chicks. Someone, or rather a group of someones, think it's something more than just a bunch of cute pictures and videos. I look across the table. He's staring at me, a weird half-smile lingering on his mouth.

"Congratulations?" he asks.

"Of course, it's congratulations!" Granna sighs, waving her hand at him. "Honestly, if I didn't really know better, I'd think you weren't paying attention to Emma and what's important to her."

My body freezes. Is she scolding him? Standing up for me? I'm stunned to say the least. He's also stunned, and now he's having the decency to be embarrassed. I can tell because his face is red, and he's stammering even more than he was a few minutes ago.

"Oh, never mind." Granna turns back to me, shaking her head in a mocking but not totally mocking scold.

"Don't mind him. He's probably just wishes he was the one off to New York City." With that, she packs up her things.

Still in shock, I hug her goodbye.

Chapter Three

Outside, he and I climb back into his truck without speaking. No amount of small talk is going to make the awkwardness go away. Most of the cornfields are nothing but rows and rows of stumps. Some still have the stalks. I watch the countryside flash by beyond the window. Funny thing to think that there are people who live beyond the cornfields. A whole different place, a whole different world. The warmth of excitement starts inside me. They picked me. There must have been a lot of entries. And… they picked me. Those people who live beyond the cornfields.

"Granna sounded pretty excited about that contest."

I slide a glance his way, but don't say anything.

"So… you're going to New York, huh?" He slows, turns a corner then accelerates, the tires humming on the asphalt. "That could be intense, ya know. Going there."

I slide him another glance, my mouth still closed as I watch his hands on the wheel. How familiar that had once been. Now it was like watching a stranger.

"I could go with you."

My mouth drops open. I snap it shut. This time I look straight at his face.

"You have to go."

Encouragement? That's a surprise. "You think I'm going to win?"

Now he looks at me, his chin dipping down, his eyebrows pulled into curls over his nose. "What? No. Yes. I mean, I don't know. That's not the point. You have to go because you told Granna you were going."

"I didn't tell her I was going."

Gaze back on the road now, he says, "You didn't tell her you weren't."

"Let me get this straight. You think I should go to New York because your grandmother, the one you're lying to about us still being together, thinks I'm going. To clarify, you think it's okay for you to lie to her but not me."

Thankfully, he stops talking for a while. I turn on the radio.

I dig out my phone, find the email, and make a screen shot of the information. I pinch into the part with the contact information and make a screen shot of that.

He turns off the radio. "Like I said, I could go with you."

"Why? Why would you want to?"

"Make sure… to make sure you're safe. It's really dangerous there. Aren't you---"

"Afraid of getting hurt?" I sneer.

He has the nerve to look surprised, and the next thing I know he's stammering again. Explaining, apologizing, and trying to convince me I need him. I had needed him, but I'd gotten over that. I hold my hand up, palm facing him. "Stop. Just stop."

"You didn't have to interrupt like that."

"Yeah. I did." I drop my hand and sigh. "Just stop talking and get me home."

After he pulls into my driveway and I climb out, I shove the door shut. The thud is heavy and final. I hear him shout "thank you" from inside his truck. I keep walking away. Away from him. Away from whatever we were. Away from who I was when I was with him. I may not know what the future is but there is one thing I do know. He's the past.

* * *

Sunday afternoon Ethan sat beside his sister on a bench in Central Park. It had been snowing since morning and the trees and walkways were lightly coated. Every few minutes, the noon sun broke through the clouds, brightening the scene but not his mood.

"You have to tell the family. The sooner the better." Beatrice paused to shake snow from her scarf, then tuck it back under the lapels of her coat.

"I will. After everything is final." They'd entered Central Park from the Columbus Circle corner and hadn't gotten three steps past the horse drawn carriages when his sister had started to pressure him into staying on in his current position. Why had he confided in her about his plan? More importantly, why couldn't she accept his decision that he wasn't the man for the job?

"How is this going to happen? You're going to invite them over for Christmas, give them all a gift, then tell them you're giving up."

It was beginning to snow harder, the air clouding with white as his mood clouded with red. "I'm not giving up."

"What about mom and dad?" She brushed snow from her hat then readjusted it.

There it was, the big issue. Why was he the one, out of the five kids, who had the sole responsibility for keeping his parent's business alive. Ethan understood, really really understood, how hard his parents worked to

23

get the agency off the ground. The two of them worked 15-hour days for years, getting the agency to the top, keeping it on the top. He knew about the long hours because he'd been the one taking care of the other four kids. Dinners. Homework. Settling arguments. Now, with both parents gone, he'd been living their life for three years now. Yes, he loved the agency, but…

"I'm not selling it. We'll still have it in the family." He hated that he sounded nearly frantic and on the verge of whiny. He wasn't the man to run the firm. He didn't have creative vision. When it came to organizing and planning, he excelled. But when it came to selecting the next big thing or understanding what made ads work, he just didn't have the knack.

That had been hard to admit to himself, let alone plan to admit to his siblings. They'd been depending on him all their lives. Still depended on him. "I know my responsibility." That was the truth.

"You won't be there every day. You won't know what's going on."

"It's called delegation. Something I'm good at."

They'd passed the playground and the snow-covered baseball fields and were headed toward Wollman Rink. It was their usual Sunday walk, crossing through the south half of the park, coming out by the zoo, then going for coffee. This was the first time he could remember feeling so out of sorts at the park. Maybe it wasn't the park. Maybe it was the conversation. Or the topic of the conversation.

"Look," she stopped to watch the skaters. "I get that you're worried about the firm, but it is doing fine. We all look at the reports and have faith in you."

Fine. Fine is okay, but he didn't want okay. He

wanted... something more. He'd been taking care of his siblings all through high school. He'd been the only undergraduate in his circle of friends to live at home. Putting their needs before his own had been automatic. Now, they were all married, three with kids, and what was he doing? Still filling someone else's footsteps. "I've been thinking about trying out one of those online dating apps." Crap. Where had that comment come from? It wasn't even close to true.

"Yes! That's a great idea! This is the perfect time of year for that." She spun in a circle as she flicked her palms outward, gesturing to the skaters, the snow-covered trees and the light covered buildings surrounding the park. "Everything is so romantic." She stopped spinning, a smile replacing the frown from a moment ago. "Want me to help you make a profile? Yes. Of course, you do. We can do it over coffee."

On second thought, blurting that out was genius. No more grilling him about staying on in a position he wasn't suited for, no more guilt about disappointing all four siblings.

How long could he stall her? Drag it out past Christmas? And New Year's? "Let's take one thing at a time. Maybe you can just explain how they work first. Then an evaluation of the qualities of each app. Then we can assess which one might suit me best. Then--"

"There's only about a week until Christmas." She grabbed his arm and pulled him away from the rink. "Now is the time to do this. Right now."

* * *

Monday morning, instead of going out to the coop to greet the girls, then checking their food and water, then

25

opening the door so they can spend their morning out in the yard, I climbed into my Jeep and drove to Detroit Metro Airport. I was through security before the sun was up. The plane shot into the sky and within minutes I was on my way. Most of the flight I stared into the clouds, trying to guess what the next few days would hold.

I'd spent most of Saturday afternoon scouring the net for information on MLNY, the ad and marketing agency, and Media Matters, the contest. I'd found a little, but not all that much. It was a boutique, exclusive family-owned and run agency that catered to other small businesses. Sunday was spent packing and walking my dad through the daily rituals involved in taking care of the birds. I'd thought a man who'd spent the last 20 years working his own dairy farm would be a bit more confident about taking care of a couple dozen chickens. Now, all that was behind me, I was getting ready to land.

I snap some selfies, pics of the clouds, and the back of the seat in front of me. These'll be good to post later. #countrychickengirl #inthecity

As the plane descends, I stare out the window, amazed, transfixed and scared. Below there's a rectangle of white, Central Park I'm guessing, surrounded by a sea of grey and brown buildings. One after the other after the other. Tall, shorter, newer, older, it's a wild mixture of everything and jam-packed with people from all around the world. We get closer to the ground, I can make out people and cars, buses and trucks. Within an hour I'll be among them. Later this afternoon, inside one of those buildings, doing the interview.

Holy crap.

Seconds later, the wheels smack the runway, and the engines roar as the plane slows.

No going back now.

Chapter Four

I'm never going to tell anyone how the morning went. Nobody would want to hear about me crying on the sidewalk, staring at the damn blue dot, walking one way, then walking the other, until finally figuring out where the hell I was. Imagine me, pulling my suitcase as it bounced over the sidewalk like a limping dog, diving into mobs of laughing, city-cool students, then popping out on the other side, still confused. It got even worse when I couldn't find the entrance to the corporate condo. Nothing from the morning was fun or camera friendly.

Once or twice, I thought of him offering to come with me, implying that I couldn't make it on my own and that I'd be in danger. The resentment that he thought I wasn't strong enough to take care of myself turned into motivation to do just that. I'd gritted my teeth and wiped my nose with the back of my hand. I made it. I got through. It just wasn't a pretty process.

None of that was Insta worthy and will forever remain a secret.

I eventually did find the corporate condo and had some time to 'collect myself.' What I really mean is wipe my face off and shake off the bad vibes.

By 1:30, I'm freshened-up, wearing the grey sweater dress, grey tights and black booties I'd selected for the interview. I'm walking toward the MLNY building. I'm no longer a total nervous wreck. In fact, I'm kind of giddy and excited.

Somehow, I'd gotten from my cow farm in Michigan to this New York City street. This morning I woke up a quaint country chicken girl. This afternoon I'm a small business owner with an interview at an ad agency. The giddiness flashes through me, and I start smiling like an idiot. Like someone who thinks they own the world.

Maybe, in this minute, I do.

I'm about 15 feet away from the huge metal framed glass doors and take it all in. Heavy strands of garland, held up with giant red bows, are wrapped around the windows stretching on either side of the doors. The building is tall and narrow. Smaller than the other buildings beside it and, from the looks of the architecture, older.

Very pretty.

Very traditional.

Almost stodgy.

I'd think an ad agency would have a more hip, cool, trendy vibe. This place looks like a bank. I double check the address. Yep. I'm in the right place. I step over and haul open one of the huge doors.

Two steps inside I stop short. The elevator is straight ahead, flanked by a row of gray and white marble columns. Garlands and potted poinsettias are everywhere. The greens are wrapped around the columns, the pots are beside the elevator doors and placed in exact locations along the walls. Classical music drifts through the air. It's very nice but also very formal. Really, kind of like a movie set. The soles of my boots hit the tile floor with a smart smack and the echo of my walk follows me as I move closer to the elevator then stop. I push the up button.

As I wait, I recognize the song. It's *Deck the Halls*, but it's barely recognizable in the very formal classical version.

Lights above blink and seconds later, the doors separate, revealing a man, standing squarely in the center of the car. He's wearing a navy-blue suit, white and blue striped shirt, and coordinating blue tie. That may sound basic, but this guy is anything but average. Everything about him says attention to detail and tailor-made. Even his face, with his deep brown eyes and perfectly positioned brown hair, looks custom made. Bespoke and perfect. When our gazes connect, I get the sensation that he's looking at me. Not a glance. He's really, really looking at me. A little something in me jumps. Well, maybe not so little. Something simmers through me, making me warm all over. Inside and out. I stand there too long, him looking at me and me staring back at him.

Me smoldering the whole time.

"Hello?" He sets his palm on one of the doors, holding it open, as he looks beyond me then back to me. "Would you like to come in?"

His smooth as butter voice snaps me out of my trance. I startle then leap into the car. "Um, thanks. Yes."

He drops his hand, smoothing his tie as he straightens. "And the floor?"

That voice again. Like hot cocoa and ginger snaps.

My heart is thumping. "Six. Sixth. Please."

"Yes, of course." He reaches across to push the button. I smell his aftershave and feel that giddiness again. But this time it's laced with something else. Some kind of drug.

There's a groaning, then the car starts moving, slowly. I'm still facing him. My mouth does a weird twitch smile which I'm beginning to fear may become my new normal. I spin around. Unfortunately, I twirl so abruptly that I bump into him. His hand goes out again, only this time to stop himself from falling.

"Are you alright?" he asks, at the same time I offer my apology.

"Yes, I—I'm fine," I say at the same time he tells me not to worry about it. That it's no problem at all.

It's all super awkward and an enormous sigh of relief rushes through me when the car bounces to a stop and the doors roll open. I hop out and hold the doors open for him.

"Oh, thank you." He glides past me. "You didn't have to—"

"Ethan. We were all set for the shoot, but the man from the agency cancelled. Something about an accident near the tunnel. Or was it the bridge? In any case, the model can't get here in time. If you want these mailed today, we must do it now. Right now. You're going to have to stand in for him." The woman rushes over, grabs the man's arm and guides him across the small lobby. Then, using both hands on his upper arms she guides him past a photo light, then positions him under an archway. A woman with a camera appears from a hallway and aims the lens at him. She spins the lens.

"Over here," she says. "This won't take long."

She's pointing to me.

"I don't think she—" he cuts her off.

"We need this done now." She's moving toward me then reaching for my arm, pulling on my coat.

"No—no," the woman with the camera interrupts. "Let's have her leave the coat on."

The closer woman tilts her head toward the man,

who's still standing in the archway. "The cards have to be printed this afternoon," she says. "If we take the photos now, the team will have just enough time to do the edits and get them out."

She sets her hands on my shoulders and guides me across the floor until I'm inches away from the man.

He looks past me, trying to get the woman's attention. "Are you sure—I don't think—"

"I know how you are about photographs. You won't be in it. At least your face won't." The woman waves to the photographer. "Alice, take them from an angle, so we just have part of her face and only part of Ethan's."

The photographer starts spinning the lens, taking a few shots as she moves closer. The light flashes each time.

"Be sure to get the mistletoe in the shot when he kisses her."

He blinks, and his entire face flashes red. I don't think I've ever seen a man blush. It is the sweetest thing ever. I glance up. A hefty sprig of twisted green leaves with white berries is dangling above.

The bossy woman sounds firm. "Really, Sir, we—"

He's taken my elbow and is speaking softly into my ear. "I'm sorry, I'll explain that—"

The guy is so mortified and anxious and embarrassed and awkward. It's adorable. I've become a new woman in only a matter of hours and miles and embrace the change. I stretch up on tiptoe and press my lips to his. Just a light peck of a kiss, but everything about it feels right.

"That's a good start." The woman is less bossy now, but still hurried. "Yes. More of that."

"Your turn," I say, looking up at him with a real

smile. Not that twitchy one from a couple minutes ago, but a real come and get me grin.

A split second later his arm is around my back, and he's holding me as he gently kisses me, pressing his lips to mine with wine-soaked perfection. I'm vaguely aware of the two women zipping about, saying how spot-on it is, just what is needed, as his mouth moves over mine, warm and firm, like flames dancing.

"That's it. We're set."

It takes some long, passion-drenched seconds for her words to sink into my hazy brain. When I pull back, he releases me. The blush is gone, replaced by an expression that gives me a different kind of wooziness.

"You aren't from the modeling agency, are you?"

"How did you know?"

"Sixth floor. We're on the fifth."

It's my turn to blush. "Oh, yeah."

He shrugs, then leans down to whisper in my ear. "I would have told them you weren't the model from the agency."

It's my turn to shrug. "I know."

"You didn't give me a chance," he says, sounding both apologetic and concerned.

"Thank you both." A voice from beyond cuts through our moment. She taps me on the shoulder. "Good work. All set. Thanks for coming."

I step toward the elevator and press the up button. "Glad to help." When I turn around, they're both gone.

They are, but he isn't.

He moves toward me, his steps long and smooth. When he stops in front of me, I think he's going to touch me again. I want him to touch me, but he simply raises a palm and gestures to the doors. I can hear them opening behind me. "Better get in, off to the sixth floor."

I take a step back. "Um, yeah. Thanks."

"No. Thank you."

I'm all jittery and shaky and giddy and have no idea what to say. I keep backing up until I'm inside the car. I hit the six button, and our gazes stay connected until the door hides him. Seconds later, the car is moving again and soon the doors glide open. I step out. There is a reception desk across the way, so I head over to check in for my interview.

Nothing, absolutely nothing, like that ever happened back home. He was totally completely different from any man I'd ever met. And me, I was a completely different person. Bonus—in a city this huge, I'll never have to see that guy again. That little moment will just be there. One random, very fun, very sexy, moment.

This city is a place where you can be yourself, try things out, and there are no consequences. Absolutely none.

Chapter Five

Forty minutes hadn't been long enough to shake the desire that moment had stirred up. He'd been kissed by many women, a few he didn't know, but the kiss from that stranger was something else. He knew that because he was back in the elevator, pulling deep breaths into his lungs, desperate for any of her scent. Was he being ridiculous? Maybe. He pulled in another breath. Citrus? Yes, whatever it was it had a touch of orange. Cloves? His mouth watered. His nerves tensed. He didn't care if he was being ridiculous.

Maybe what he was experiencing was some sort of after effect from the deluge of responses he'd received after Bea made that dating profile. He should've stopped his sister from creating it, but after the way she'd instantly abandoned her plan to convince him to stay on at his current job, he'd found himself sitting there like an idiot, sipping coffee while he answered questions, and then agreeing to the pictures she selected off his Facebook profile. Now, every time he looked in the app, there were responses from more and more beautiful women. Who knew there were so many in the city? Some of the women seemed nice enough, educated, fun and interesting. He'd thought about writing back to a few, but after 15 minutes of scrolling through, all the faces blurred together.

That woman under the mistletoe was different. She was real. And *she'd* kissed *him*.

Get a grip, he told himself as he stepped out of the elevator car, heading to the conference room in the back of the sixth-floor office suite. Just one more interview today, then he'd meet with the accountant to finalize everything. Four more days, and he'd be out of there. He made his way through the maze of desks and tables. Staff he didn't know, nodded or said hello as he passed by. Truth be told, he'd been withdrawing from the agency for months now. Finalizing the status was past due. All he had to do was get through these last few days. How tough could that be?

He flipped open the first file of the stack. The details of the contestants were laid out in neat columns. There were stats about Instagram—columns about stories and followers. There was some analysis on engagement and reach. Inwardly, he sighed. His NYU MBA had not prepared him for this. He probably should just give the stack to Carlson's sister, Lina, ask her to tell him which of these five people was going to be the next big influencer.

A murmur of voices drifted to him, reaching him before he got to the door. He paused. It wasn't conversation. His staff was laughing. Actually laughing. He closed the folder, then tucked it under his arm. No one told him these interviews were supposed to be fun.

He glanced down at his suit jacket, smoothed out his tie, considered his pants.

More laughter rolled out into the hallway.

Were his shoes too shiny? Too tightly-laced? Why was he feeling so overdressed?

According to his watch, he was already two minutes late. He went in.

The room was arranged in the same configuration as the previous two interviews. Tom and Shakira, the two running the contest, were on one side of the long conference table, a view of the city behind them. An empty chair on the end, closest to the door, had been left vacant for him. Across the table from his staff, a screen hung from the ceiling. A computer workstation was to the right of the screen. The computer there projected whatever the interviewee had running on their laptop.

The two times before this one, he'd simply gone in, nodded his hello, then took his seat to observe. The agreement he'd made with Tom and Shakira was that he'd listen and be present but not participate. It wasn't that he didn't want to put the effort in. It was that he understood his limitations. When it came to social media and what was going to be the next big thing, he had no skill. Now, he was regretting that arrangement. Especially the non-participating part.

The woman at the front of the room was bent over, clicking through a series of posts. Even with her face hidden, he knew instantly who she was. A bolt of awareness shot through his body. She described aspects of images, his staff still laughing lightly. Even Shakira, usually all business, was smiling. None of them had noticed him come in. That was a good thing because he was having a hard time walking normally. Never mind what must have become of his face.

Starting to stand, Miss Mistletoe continued, "One of my recent stories included a link to—"

Then their gazes connected, and it was just as powerful and electric as when they'd been inches apart in the archway. All at once he could feel the soft press of her mouth and smell that citrusy scent. Less than an hour ago, he'd had his arms around her. He shouldn't, but he wanted that again. No, he understood now, her presence wasn't just as powerful. It was more powerful.

Shakira and Tom gradually stopped laughing, their faces turning from the image on the screen, a trio of chickens sitting inside some kind of shelf contraption. Miss Mistletoe, still half bent over, was gradually starting to stand, her just-kissed mouth forming words but no sound coming out.

"Hello," he said, pretending to be relaxed and at ease.

She straightened the rest of the way, and her long brown hair settled around her shoulders. "Hello."

"Chickens," he said, pointing to the screen.

"Yes, that's right. Chickens." She gestured to the giant size photo beside her. "I raise chickens and sell..."

"... I see that." He stepped further into the room. "They're... they're..." He should say something positive, but what positive words described chickens? And now he was standing awkwardly, halfway into the room, with his hands dangling at his sides, his heart thumping, and his face turning red.

"Ethan? Are you coming in to join us?" Shakira pointed to the empty seat that'd been left for him. "Ms. Lopez sells supplies to chicken farmers. Even to people in the city."

"This city?" he choked out, looking to the window.

She nodded; her deep brown eyes fixed on him. "That's right."

He pointed to the maze of buildings. "People, here— in New York—have chickens?"

Ms. Lopez nodded, her reply matter of fact and sure. "Hens only though. Roosters are illegal."

37

He'd never seen any chickens in the city. He'd lived there is whole life and never seen one. Except maybe at the petting zoo. Ms. Mistletoe was pretty and sexy. But maybe a bit crazy too. "Roosters are illegal. Hens are okay. That's what you're telling me?"

"Yes." Full of confidence and charm, she replied. "That's right."

He pulled himself together, nodded, even though he still thought she was nuts, and took a seat. "I see. Well. Thank you. Please. Continue."

While she started talking again, he flipped open the second folder and skimmed through the pages. Miss Mistletoe, Emma Lopez, continued talking, clicking through her images and describing her approach to using Instagram posts and stories as well as other social media. He had to admit, her posts were eye catching. Bright colors, a homey but upbeat sophisticated sense to them. He could tell they were good, but he'd never be able to explain why.

"Ms. Lopez, would it surprise you to know that Ethan," Tom pointed to him, "doesn't think much of Instagram?"

The man had made the same comment in the two previous interviews, but this time he noticed it made him sound like a small-minded idiot. What kind of ad exec says that sort of thing?

"I don't think it's completely useless," he said, closing the folder.

A quirky smile pulled on Emma's mouth. "Is that right? Then why are you here?"

He liked that she was challenging him, and wished desperately for a snappy come back, but only came up with the obvious. "I work here."

Shakira was chuckling again. Once she stopped, she said, "We have him here to tamp down on the excitement."

Tom smiled over at Ethan. "We have him here because he's the boss."

She tensed for just the briefest second, then her smile broadened. "Well then. I'm glad you're here." With that, she began describing her approach to connecting with an audience. He tried to listen, really, he did. But apparently, he'd turned into one of those men who saw a pretty face and an appealing body and blanked out. To be fair, it was a body he'd been touching less than an hour ago. Attached to a woman he'd been kissing. Or getting started kissing. Damn.

Fortunately, they'd all agreed he wouldn't have any input on selecting the winner. He trusted Tom and Shakira's judgment. All he had to do was sit tight and wait this meeting out. Then he'd go to his accountant as planned, take care of everything with the final arrangements, and go home. Or go for a walk. Maybe get a drink, then walk through the park. Or do some shopping.

"Right Ethan? Doesn't that sound like a good idea?"

He looked up. "Umm…"

"Just say yes," Shakira offered, grinning. "You said you'd trust the process."

What, exactly, did she mean by that?

Tom leaned forward, an odd gleam in his eyes. "That's right. Here's your chance to prove it."

Miss Mistletoe's gaze was zeroed in on him, her face a mixture of anticipation and something else. Excitement? Dread? Longing? Distaste? While he was staring at her, her eyebrows raised. There was that challenge again.

He had no choice but to agree. "Yes, of course."

"Great. I checked your schedule." Shakira tapped her nails on the tabletop. "You're free the rest of the afternoon."

"You sure? He's free all afternoon?" Tom opened his laptop, started clicking as he glanced at Shakira. "How is that possible?"

Shakira shrugged at Tom, then looked at Ethan. "You're free, right?"

One thing, he had no idea what he agreed to, but he already knew it was a bad idea. He wasn't creative but he did have intuition. Second thing, he couldn't tell them why he had blocked off the time that afternoon.

"Yep. You're free." Tom closed his laptop. "Guess it's just slow because next week is Christmas."

Shakira folded her hands. "It's a go then."

Miss Mistletoe unplugged her laptop, closed it, then stashed it into her bag. "Four o'clock work for you?"

He tried to read her expression, but again it was an indecipherable mixture. Not that it made any difference, he had agreed to whatever it is that he'd agreed to. "Sure. Great."

She crossed the room, came around to the window side of the table and offered her hand first to Shakira and then to Tom, thanking them both for their time and attention. When she reached him, she hitched the bag onto her shoulder and asked, "Meet out front?"

How about we meet in the elevator again? Thankfully he just thought that and managed not to say it aloud.

"Yes, out front will be fine." He offered his hand, then tried not to hold hers too long when they shook. A minute later, she was gone.

Chapter Six

At exactly 4:00, he steps out one of the giant doors, walks straight to me. Since getting over the shock of seeing him stroll into the interview, I've decided to own that kiss. I did it. I enjoyed it. And I didn't feel bad about it. I also understood it meant I was probably not going to win the contest.

"You don't know what you agreed to, do you?" I asked him once he'd stopped in front of me.

"That obvious?" he said he replied with a shrug.

He was wearing a perfectly fitted cashmere overcoat and looking even more handsome than he had earlier that morning. This time, though, he was smiling and looking very much at ease. No red flush of embarrassment. No awkward nervousness. "You aren't going to tell me, are you?" he asked, buttoning up his coat.

I take a sheet a of paper from my pocket and offer it to him. "How about I give you the address, you get us there."

He glances at the address. "I'll get us a car."

The subway was an adventure, but I'm happy to not do that again so soon. "How we get there is up to you."

He slips his phone from his chest pocket, taps the screen. "Should only be a minute or two.'

We stand side by side, watching the traffic stream

by. The sidewalk is crowded and busy, people zipping in both directions. I watch them cruise by, stepping quickly but never bumping into each other. Off in the distance, maybe it's coming from across the street, bells are jangling. The air is scented with roasted chestnuts, which, I have discovered, don't smell very good. Still, I'm mesmerized.

He slides his phone into his inner chest pocket, the movement smooth and graceful and somehow filled with confidence. "Have you been having a nice visit?"

"I think so." He must have seen my expression. There's no hiding my awe. "I only got here this morning."

He nods. I smile. He smiles back. The whole thing would be hilarious if it were in a movie, but because it isn't, I'm not laughing. I'm zinging with excitement and anxious to do the right thing. Whatever that is.

Thankfully, the car pulls up and rolls to a stop at the curb. We hurry over and climb in, only to be seated side by side, and again, trying to fill the weird silence. The drive across the bridge into Brooklyn takes a while, but Ethan had been talking to the driver about traffic and sports, so I had time to gaze out the window. The driver pulls up in front of a brick building. We climb out and I send a message to Sammi.

Seconds later, a man erupts from a door.

"Oh. My. God. It's you! It's really you!" Sammi charges down the steps, arms wide, and hauls me into a bear hug. He's over six feet tall, with a massive chest and a shaved head. He's holding me so tightly that my feet are off the ground, and I can't breathe that easily, but other than that the greeting is the sweetest welcome I've known in a while.

He sets me down, his hands on my shoulders. "The

Chicken Chick. Right here in Brooklyn. At my apartment. Right here."

I'm laughing now. That's a new one. "The Chicken Chick?"

Ethan is looking a little lost, his gaze zipping back and forth between Sammi and me. Sammi is wearing blue jean overalls and a red and green plaid flannel shirt and looking the total opposite of buttoned up Ethan.

I gesture over. "This is Ethan. His ad agency is the reason I'm here in the city."

Sammi grabs Ethan and pulls him into a hug. Squeezing him, he says, "Thank you, thank you, thank you. You are the best. The absolute best."

He lets go, sets Ethan back, still smiling. "You both have to come in and meet my roomie, Ilsa. You just have to meet her. She only speaks Spanish. Go ahead and talk to her, but she won't have much idea what you're saying. Well, she'll have some idea, because I told her you were coming, by drawing a picture." He flattens his hand on his chest and laughs. "I know. I know. But it works. She's only been here a couple days. Came from Guatemala." He looks Ethan over, taking in his overcoat and shiny shoes. "You aren't a MAGA person or anything, are you? From ICE? I mean, she's not from *a caravan* or anything."

Ethan shakes his head. I don't know exactly what he's saying no to, but it's clear to me he's telling Sammi that despite his polished and affluent appearance he isn't any kind of threat.

Sammi grabs my hand, waves at Ethan with the other, then pulls me toward his building.

Once we're through the door, he jogs ahead, then stops at a door at the end of the hall. "Come on. Come in," Sammi says over his shoulder as he opens the door. "Meet Ilsa first. Then you have to see the girls." He sweeps the door open. "Oh. My. God. You're actually here. So awesome."

Ethan is coming, his stride smooth and even. I wonder if he knows how out of place he looks in his suit and dress coat. He's grinning, though, which is a surprise.

"Okay?" I ask him once he's beside me.

"This is the most fun I've had in a while."

Not what I was expecting him to say. This buttoned up guy I don't really know, but have kissed under the mistletoe, is completely different than any guy I've ever met. Too bad I'm not going to see him any more after this week.

Sammi steps into the apartment and calls out, "Ilsa, she's here. And there's a guy with her."

He glances at me and shrugs, as if to say, it's only polite to talk to someone even if they can't understand what you're saying. Makes sense to me. Judging by the look on Ethan's face it makes sense to him too.

The inside of Sammi's apartment is a crazy splash of color. Yellow, red, orange, ice blue and white. The walls are covered with vintage style prints of the city, all framed in white. The coffee table in front of the denim-covered couch is stacked with books about chickens and farms. A dark-haired woman wearing an oversize beige sweater and jeans comes into the cozy front room from the kitchen nook. She waves to me, then to Ethan.

When Sammi introduces us, and we say hello, I notice her watching my lips, the same way some of my dad's friends do. My dad never caught on to lip reading, signing worked better for him, maybe because he's a hands-on kind of guy.

Sammi starts talking about his chickens, and she's watching his mouth. I start telling him about my girls, and she's watching my mouth.

It's possible she's hearing impaired, but it sure seems like Sammi would have mentioned it. Well, maybe not. Maybe she doesn't want anyone to know? Maybe Sammi doesn't know.

"Let's go see the chickens." Sammi is up and moving through the narrow kitchen nook to a back door. I follow. Ethan follows me and Ilsa follows us all. "This way, out here." Sammi opens the door, then pauses and holds one palm up. "Promise me we can do some selfies. We have to do the selfies."

"Of course, we will."

Ethan has a weird half-smile lingering on his mouth, almost like he's watching a skit. But he's paying attention and it's sweet and kind and makes my heart skip a beat.

I follow Sammi outside onto his cozy patio. A black and white hen is pecking through the little bit of snow covering the brick. Her black and white stripes and bright red comb are beautiful against the small heaps of snow piled on the railings behind her.

I take out my camera. "Can I take a picture?"

Sammi is thrilled. "Yes, yes, of course."

I snap a photo of her as a sweet little silkie scurries out from the small coop a few feet from where the patio ends. The coop is painted bright red and tucked under a gnarled fruit tree. Once she's closer, I see that the little hen is sporting a green and white sweater.

A sweater!

Her fluffy wing feathers are poking out of the cabled 'arm' holes.

"Sammi! Did you knit that?"

He nods, smug and beaming. "I did. I have silver ones for New Year's."

Two Rhode Island Reds follow her out, their rust colored feathers bright against the grey snow-cloud sky. I'm a little disappointed that they don't have sweaters, but then a richly black Maran, cozy in a white and red sweater appears from behind the coop. Sammi is gushing about his hens, and I'm snapping pictures. Then he starts taking pictures too. Then Ethan gets his phone out. The next thing I know, we're all taking pictures of each other, ourselves, the birds, and everything in Sammi's quaint backyard. I'm posting pics, tagging Sammi and, with Ethan's okay, MLNY.

Sammi and I gush over the fashionable chicken sweaters, then explode with laughter at our hashtag #birdsandthecity. Ethan has no idea what we're referring to and that makes us laughter even harder. So hard I have to wipe my eyes.

Still laughing, Sammi gathers us all up and shoos us back inside for some tea. He seats us on the couch, then goes to get the drinks prepared. By this time, I'm certain Ilsa is reading our lips. Or trying to read our lips. And she isn't making a secret of it.

I catch her eye, then raise my hands to sign, *I just got here today. How do you like the city?*

And just like that, she's 'talking.'

While Ethan watches, mouth still and sort of hanging open, I find out a couple things.

By the time Sammi joins us, she and I are fully into a conversation. After asking her if it's okay if I share what she says, I fill Sammi in on what I find out. Her sister is staying across the street, Sammi confirms, and she loves the city and wants to go to school. She lived in LA for three years, learned American Sign Language there and is still trying to lip read English. She has two brothers and knows nothing about chickens.

I tell her I'm from the country and know nothing about the city. She laughs. I laugh too. The whole thing is a blur, but still I have time to notice Ethan, watching. I don't know if I can describe the expression on his handsome face. Curious, yes, that's one thing. Surprised… I could go so far as to say shocked.

That scene outside, with the chickens, was something new, I can tell. It's like he's never seen anyone making posts before. When he'd started asking questions, it was obvious he barely even understood social media. By the time we're saying goodbye, he's looking thoroughly confused but also excited. Maybe that's why he asked me if I wanted to go to dinner with him. To finish explaining. About the social media. Not to explain about the kiss.

Chapter Seven

An hour later, Ethan was seated across the table from Emma. He'd suggested his favorite Italian restaurant for dinner. It was a cozy place, with intimate little tables with low candles on the tables. It was a Monday night, so there was a mix of friends, families and only a few couples.

After the server brought the wine and filled their glasses, she sat back, her face still flushed from the chilly winter air. "There's something I need to ask."

He opened his jacket and settled back. "Yes, of course."

"Are you taking the other finalists out to dinner?"

Her question made sense. He probably should've explained his involvement, or lack of it, in the contest earlier. "I don't think so. No plans to."

She nodded, but her expression stayed slightly guarded. "You understand why I'm asking. Right?"

Her question reflected her professionalism. That kiss for the photograph had been impulsive, but it also been part of her personal life. She hadn't known who he was at the time. Now that she did, things were complicated, but not in the way that she was worried about. "I made an agreement with Tom and Shakira. I have no influence over the contest winner."

She picked up her wine glass, swirled it. "None?"

"None at all." He shook his head. "Shakira came up with the contest concept. She and Tom developed it. I haven't had any real input from the start."

She took a sip of the wine and smiled over the top of the glass. "That's probably a good thing."

"It is a good thing. It means I don't have to feel bad about having a good time right now. Neither do you." After she set the glass down, he asked, "Tell me more about the chickens."

Her mouth twisted. "You aren't serious."

"I am." He leaned back, nodding. "Tell me more."

"Like what? What could I possibly tell you?"

"Anything."

Her smirk made his stomach flip.

"Hens lay eggs." She said. "How's that for information?"

"You said roosters are illegal here in the city."

"Makes sense to me. I'm guessing it's because they're noisy. And mean."

"Mean?"

"If there is more than one, especially."

"So, no roosters in all of New York."

"Not unless they're here illegally."

"But… but…"

She lifted an eyebrow, that sexy quirky smirk tugging on her mouth. Her thoughtful and challenging expression was so much better than the vacant smiles of the dozens of faces he'd scanned through in that app. Many of those women were beautiful, but now he realized they didn't look like someone he could hold a conversation with over dinner. He went ahead and asked the thing that had been on his mind all afternoon. "What about the eggs?"

"What about them?" she asked in reply, confusion filling her eyes.

"How… how…" All at once, he had the feeling he was in the middle of asking a stupid question.

"What?" she asked, tipping her head to look at him in a sideways glance.

He shifted in his chair. There was no backing out now. "How do the hens lay eggs without…" But he couldn't go on because her sideways glance was turning slightly evil, in the cutest possible way, of course.

She let him hang there, awkward and turning red, until she finally filled in his silence with a question. "Without roosters?"

Now he was certain he'd asked a dumb question, but for the life of him he couldn't figure out why it was stupid. He just knew it was. Too late now, though, because she was already grinning at his expense. At first, she tried to hide her laughter, but soon it was spilling out sideways, her shoulders shaking, tears in her eyes.

"Thank you." She said between breaths. "I needed that."

He watched her toss her long curls out of her eyes, exposing a new flush in her cheek. "Glad to," he replied, meaning it even though she was totally laughing at him. He'd been laughed at before, but never in a way that made him feel this way. Warm. Happy.

After a long breath exhaled, she looked at him from the corner of her eyes. "You really don't know, do you."

No getting out of it. "Nope. I don't."

"You think the hens needs roosters to lay eggs?"

He shrugged one shoulder.

She lifted her eyebrows.

He nodded.

"They don't. The hens don't need the roosters. They just don't."

His mouth twisted. She started laughing again, looked side to side as she leaned toward him then waited for him to do the same. Once he leaned in, she whispered. "Women all around you produce eggs all the time, every month, without the assistance from men." She leaned back and let that sink in.

It did.

She started laughing again, probably at the shock and embarrassment on his face, and he started laughing too. Good grief, how ridiculous.

"I thought… I really did think…"

Still laughing, she waved her hands to cut him off. "No more, please, I can't take it."

Thankfully, their food arrived, saving him from his own ridiculousness. Throughout the meal, he asked her more questions about her social media accounts and the ways she interacted with people online. Throughout it all, she gave him the information he requested, but delivered it with a touch of humor.

Over dessert she asked him about his job and family. Usually, he dodged the questions about how he started running the company, but telling Emma the truth, that he'd inherited it from his parents, seemed natural. Most times when a woman asked him how he got his start, he felt lame telling them about how he stepped into the role so easily. He had no hard luck, scrapping his way to the top through hard work and innate talent, tale to show off his skills and manliness. The stories about raising his four siblings while both his parents worked weren't so glamorous or masculine either. Bragging about being able to change diapers and pack lunches didn't impress most women. Emma was different. She smiled at his accounts of epic meal failures and pretending to be his dad when calling in sick for his little brothers or sisters. Being an only child, she knew nothing about sibling rivalry or the power of love-hate relationships.

By the time he dropped her off at the corporate condo, he was very, very glad he had no input on the winner. His judgment was not objective. But he was smiling for the first time, he realized now, in a long time.

* * *

Having dinner with Ethan made me giddy in a way I've never felt. Even after I changed into my leggings and T-shirt, I was still vibrating with energy. I skimmed through the pictures I'd taken at Sammi's, posted some more and started a New York photo album on Facebook. It's too late to Facetime my dad, so I start flipping through Netflix and am bombarded with Christmas movies. *Baby Comes for Christmas*, *Christmas at Harmony Ranch*, *Countdown to Christmas*, and my personal fave, *Country for Christmas*. There must be something wrong with me because I don't want any of these versions of Christmas. No baby, no church choir and no country men. My finger hovers over that last offering. A woman from Seattle gives up her successful real estate business to move into a quaint bed and breakfast in the country because she feels like she's lost the spirit of Christmas. Then she meets a farmer who solves all her problems and teaches her that living simply and scraping to get by is what life is truly about.

Oh dear. I've turned kind of snarky.

My finger is still over the play now tab. Why? I ask myself. Why would I want to put myself through that?

Why isn't there a *Pitch Perfect* Christmas movie?

More importantly, how can I get back to that all-over giddy sensation I had when I stepped into this lovely corporate condo?

The answer to that is obvious. Think about Ethan. His sexy brown eyes. The casual way he smooths back his hair. The crisp fit of his burgundy dress shirt.

Does he own anything besides dress shirts?

I try to imagine him wearing jeans and fall asleep, smiling.

Chapter Eight

I spent all of Tuesday morning burning off nervous energy. The contest event for the afternoon is going to be a meet and greet with the other finalists. Will they all be Instagram users? Will they be older? Younger? Will any of them be country people like me? Will I feel like a fraud? Inept? Will I know immediately after meeting them that I'm not a contender?

See what I mean about that nervous energy?

I went to The Met, then walked along the park. I ate a hot dog from a cart. I bought a couple postcards I may or may not get around to sending. I took a picture of a Santa on his lunch break. I took pictures of dogs getting walked in the park. I took the subway and didn't get lost and now I'm in front of the building, again. Just as anxious as I had been yesterday.

Seriously, though, maybe more nervous.

What if Ethan told Tom and Shakira about that kiss?

He wouldn't, would he?

What would be the benefit?

I straighten the straight plaid skirt I'd picked out for day two and march myself toward the doors. I'll hold my head up, try not to kiss anyone, and concentrate on being fun and smart. Lively and creative. Someone who belongs there.

Yes. I can do that.

My heels echo on the tiles as I move toward the elevator. That same formal Christmas music is playing. I glance at the garlands as I pass them, then push the up button. The doors glide open. The car is empty this time. Soon, the doors open on the sixth floor and I step out. More Christmas music, a jazzy version of *Let It Snow*. Better than the classical, but not all that great. I wave at the guy behind the reception desk. He waves, then tips his head toward the conference room.

"All the way in the back. Same as yesterday," he says before turning his attention to the monitor on his desk. I head down the hall, then step into the room.

It's a small but chatty group, and nobody notices me when I come in.

Butterflies flutter in my stomach as I stand there, holding my laptop bag strap, suddenly shy and intimidated. Across the room, I spot a guy standing alone, about the same age as me, also looking lost and alone but also anxious and full of energy like a kid after a week of camp.

He's buff and beautiful. He's wearing a fitted, tight, black T-shirt and some kind of pants that aren't quite sweats but aren't quite pants either. His shoes have a thick sole, but I doubt he's wearing them to make himself taller. He's over six feet and from the looks of him every inch is muscle. Even his hair is perfect in a tousled, I-just-got-done-at-the-gym, kind of way. While I'm staring at him, he runs his hand through the messy styled stuff, then digs his phone out of his pocket. I don't know why, but I feel like I know him. He looks familiar, yes, but there's no way I'd know a guy like him and not be able to place him within seconds. Every guy I know lives in flannels and feed store T-shirts. I don't think this guy has ever even touched either, let alone put them on his chiseled body.

55

Then he gets out his phone, raises it and snaps a series of selfies. Within seconds he's made his selection, posted it, and slid his phone back into his front left pocket. His gaze is back on the group scanning, his body vibrating with energy. Then it dawns on me—I don't actually know him, but I've seen him on Instagram. Of course, he's one of the finalists.

I weave between the group, trying to make eye contact as I get closer. It doesn't work. I stop right in front of him. "Hi."

He shifts his perfect looking face in my direction but doesn't say anything.

"Hi," I say again. "Nice to meet you. I think we're here for the same reason."

One of his beautiful eyebrows lifts.

"You're here for the contest, right? You're a finalist?" Ugh. My Midwestern twang just showed up, making me sound like the country girl I am.

He looks me up and down, his gaze pausing on my laptop bag before coming back to my face.

I look at my bag, then back to him. "I'm here for the contest too."

"Hey," someone is tapping me on the shoulder. "You're a finalist?"

I turn to find an older woman, in her 50's I'd guess, wearing a navy-blue tracksuit with white piping. Yes, the pants and jacket match. Yes, it really, really looks like she's been wearing it since 1994. But hey, at least she's acting like a human.

"I am." I point to him. "I think he is too."

He's watching the clusters of people around the room.

She holds out her hand and speaks firmly. "Marilyn

Caldwell." I shake her hand and offer my own name, then add, "I sell chicken supplies for urban farming. You know, a drop ship sort of thing."

"Excellent." She turns to the guy. "What's your gig?"

"My gig?" he replies, turning toward us and putting emphasis on the second word.

"I think she means your thing that you do," I offer with a shrug.

Beside me now, she nods.

"I am a fitness influencer. I promote healthy lifestyles."

And perfect male beauty, I add to myself.

Marilyn nods her approval. "I'm a motivation speaker. I inspire success and self-control."

Oh. Intriguing mixture. I wonder why she'd separated them out. Like a person can have one without the other or needs both. I think about asking her, but she is in actuality, pretty intimidating. Everything about her screams confidence. Even in that vintage track suit, she's a total take charge person. I guess that's why she is a motivator.

She lifts her hand to her brow and scans the room. "I think that one over there is a finalist too." Pointing, she jabs her finger to the right. Sure enough, there is a guy standing off to the side looking bewildered and alone. I hadn't spotted him before because he's almost hiding behind the Christmas tree.

"Come on, folks," she calls waving us to follow her as she plows straight ahead, people dodging on either side as she splits the crowd with just her presence and will. I follow her and, surprisingly, the fitness guy follows me.

We circle the guy behind the tree and say hello. When we ask if he's a finalist, he nods silently. He's holding a Christmas tree cookie that is completely covered in red and green sprinkles. He has yet to take a bite from it.

Marilyn is leaning towards me, eyes big with excitement. "Thrilling opportunity, isn't it?"

"Sure is. Do you know what else we're doing today?" I hate revealing my ignorance, but I hate even more not knowing what's going on.

"This is all I know too." She puts her hands on her hips and swivels, scanning the room.

I tap Fitness Guy on the shoulder. "Do you know—"

But before I can finish, the guy moves from behind the Christmas tree and points the cookie to a beautiful woman who'd just come in the room. "I think she's the last one of us." "Excellent." Marilyn says. She turns to the three of us, then gestures over her shoulder. "Come on, folks."

I follow her. The guy from behind the tree is behind me, and I assume fitness guy is behind him.

We arrive in front of the woman and semi-circle her like a mismatched quartet.

"Hi," I offer my hand. She introduces herself as Nula.

"What's your gig," Fitness Guy asks.

Marilyn smiles. I smile. Tree Guy looks confused but happy.

The five of us exchange basics and soon I know fitness guy's real name, Flynn, the guy from behind the tree is Carl, Cannabis Carl actually, and our newcomer, Nula, is a beauty influencer. That explains her flawless face and hair. The rest of her is perfect too.

We discuss how we've been getting around and what we've done besides get lost and prepare for our one-on-one interviews which we're all done with now. Then we all figure out that we're staying in the same building, just on different floors. About the time we're telling each other the best places to eat near our building, Shakira comes over and asks us all to move to the wide wall across from the windows for pictures.

Still chatting, we move across the room in a cluster. As we're walking, I'm looking between people to see if Ethan is around somewhere, but he's not. Him not being there is a good thing, I tell myself. I won't be distracted, and it proves what he said is true. He's not involved in selecting the winner.

Marilyn, Carl and Flynn are the three in the back. Nula and I are in the front.

Once Shakira has us arranged, she steps back and gestures. The photographer makes her way toward us. My heart literally stops when her gaze connects with mine.

Simultaneously, she lowers the camera and her mouth drops open. She's staring hard at me, her eyes reflecting the whirl that must be taking place in her mind.

I look over at Nula, desperately trying to think of something to say, but come up blank. She notices me looking at her. She smiles awkwardly. I smile back, then look back to the photographer.

"Are we positioned okay?" I ask. "Do you want anyone to move? The light okay?"

"It's—it's fine." She raises the camera, her fingers curling around the barrel of the lens. The first clicks of the camera catch everyone's attention, and they all stop talking. My heart is thumping now, but I think the moment has passed. She either hasn't figured out why I look familiar, or she's decided to not call me out on my questionable behavior of the day before.

I breathe a sigh of relief and smile.

After the group picture is done, we each get an individual portrait. Then Shakira gathers us together again, standing before us with a gleeful but slightly evil grin.

"Now, for the challenge."

Chapter Nine

Marilyn is the first to respond. She's put her hands on her hips. "Let me at it."

Nula fluffs her hair. Flynn nods.

Cannabis Carl mumbles, "Yeah, dude. Cool and stuff."

"We'll be roaming around the city, visiting some of the usual tourist spots, waiting to see what unusual things you all can do with them."

My mind starts spinning. It seems doubtful that we're going anywhere where there will be chickens, barns or country stuff. I know nothing of the city. Crap. I don't even know what the usual tourist spots are.

Marilyn already has her phone in her hands. "When will we be in the park?" she wants to know.

Tom steps forward, sheets of paper in his hand.

As soon as he hands one to Marilyn, she scans it over. Within seconds her fingers are a flurry over her phone.

"The only rule for the challenge is that we have to keep to the time schedule."

I look over the list. We end at Central Park. We start at a park called Washington Square. Then to the Empire State Building, Rockefeller Center, a surprise spot, then Central Park.

Marilyn is the only one of us who looks like she knows what to do. She's clicking and tapping, her firm mouth in a steady sure position. I pull my phone out and stare at the locked screen. Louisa's black eyes stare at me from the glossy surface. Do something, her gaze says.

"We're going to five places." I say, looking at the four others circled around me. "There are five of us."

Carl pulls his phone out and sets it on the table. "Dude. That's radical."

Marilyn is nodding. The others are staring blankly, probably feeling as lost and confused as I am. "How about we highlight one of us at each location? Take pictures of one person, mostly, and cross post."

There's a beat of quiet, then Marilyn lowers her phone. "Excellent plan. Perfect way to build momentum. The park for me."

Flynn lifts his hand. "Empire State Building."

Nula does a little shimmy. "The surprise spot."

"You cool with Rockefeller Center?" Carl asks me. "I heard of that Washington Square Park. It," he pretends to straighten a tie he's probably never worn then changes his tone to what must pass for him as a serious businessperson. "It aligns with my brand identity." He drops his hand, his voice again sounding vaguely buzzed. "At least I think it might. It did at one time." He looks at Tom, "Is the city still clean like that?"

"That park is a hangout place for the NYU kids."

"Cool. I know it's a different world out there now, but one thing never changes. College kids dig weed." He pats his chest. "And weed icons."

This is the most Carl has said at once, and his attitude is exactly what we need to lighten the mood. Nula starts to giggle. Flynn follows, also giggling. Marilyn guffaws, then the rest of us join in. Carl is laughing too, until he starts to cough. That makes the rest of us laugh harder, and soon I have to wipe tears from my cheeks.

Minutes later, the seven of us are packed into the elevator, now laughing at the overformal classical Christmas music. No, it isn't that funny. But we're all laughing anyway.

It goes that way the next couple hours.

At Washington Square Park, Carl grabs a man wearing a purple NYU DAD sweatshirt and does a series of selfies. Then he does some selfies with a couple cops he finds drinking coffee near the fountain. The rest of us cheer him on. I add a live feed of him to my Insta story, hashtagging and tagging him and everyone else. Cross branding at it's finest. Next thing I know, the others are doing the same and our stories and follows are moving up at lightning speed. After we all pose in front of the Christmas tree under the arch, we climb into the Uber van and head off.

The next stop is the Empire State Building. Before we go inside, Flynn talks a pedicab driver into lending him his pedicab. He insists we do close-ups of his chiseled calves and full body pics from every angle. I have to admit, he does look beautiful and the folks on my feed love him, hearting him up within seconds of the posts. After exhausting the merits of the pedicab, Tom and Shakira take us all the way up to the 102nd floor. There is a gush of amazement followed by another round of photos. The sun is sliding lower over the city, sending long shadows over the buildings. The lights are just beginning to brighten the grey, winter sky. While we are absorbing one last look, Tom ushers us out of the observatory and on to our next stop.

Nula's surprise spot turns out to be the Russian Tea room. The five of us slide into one of the semi-circular red booths and instantly feel like movie stars. Or, to be accurate, social media stars. The gold and red background is the perfect backdrop for Nula's blonde hair. After taking pictures, we sag back, make a no pics while eating pact, and chow on the delicious tiny sandwiches. Warmed up from the tea and champagne, we ramble back out into the dark, winter evening and stuff ourselves into the van.

Flynn is the first one to spot the tree at Rockefeller Center. I bend down to peek at it through the window. I'm speechless. It must be wrapped with a million lights. Sneaky Shakira, who has planned all of the stops to run like clockwork, has already gotten our shoe sizes and planned ahead for us to have skates. I thank the luck Gods because ice skating is something I can do. Everyone snaps pics and videos of me as I zip around the rink, weaving between scarf-wrapped children and tumbling teenagers. After we change back into our own footwear, Tom gets us some hot cocoa from a food cart.

"The park isn't far, so we're walking from here," he tells us.

Sipping from our steaming cups, we start moving, taking pictures and making videos as we walk past the sparkling, holiday-perfect buildings. The chilly night air is heavy with the city smells, exhaust, roasted peanuts, smoke, dirt and other scents I can't identify. It's nearly impossible to keep the awestruck expression off my face. I can't believe this is my life, but it is. It's only been two days, but already I feel at home on the sidewalks, crossing the jam-packed streets as though I'd been born there. Dodging yellow cabs as they creep around the corner is nothing new to me.

"Where is Times Square?" Flynn wants to know.

Tom and Shakira exchange looks, then simultaneously point back generally toward the direction we'd come from.

"Are we going to see it?" he asks.

They exchange glances, then look at Flynn, both shaking their heads firmly. "Don't go there," they say in unison then laugh.

"I want to go there," he insists.

Marilyn puts her hand on his arm. "The park is going to be all you need."

He looks at her, doubtful.

"Trust me," she says, then turns forward, marching north. "This is going to rock."

Like ducks on the way to the pond, the four of us follow Marilyn. Tom and Shakira trail behind us, taking shots of our group on the streets doing all the usual touristy things. Nula buys a scarf from a vendor. I dig through, but ultimately pass on, some counterfeit bags. Flynn watches his reflection move in the large shop windows, and Carl floats along, mumbling pleasantly to no one in particular and smiling vaguely.

When we reach the edge of the park, Marilyn stops short, hands on her hips and shoulders back. We stop behind her, scanning the walkways leading into the park even though we don't know what we're looking for. She gestures to the left, starting to walk again, and we pick up behind her, marching along, my anticipation and curiosity growing as we cross the last street before reaching the park.

It is as dark as it probably gets in the city, so the lights from the horse draw carriages twinkle. The lampposts glow, casting warm shadows on the walks that lead deeper into the park. As we move closer, I see that some of the trees are wrapped in tiny white lights. Nula waves to the horses now behind us and starts singing *Jingle Bells*, and we all join in. The bare trees are coated with a layer of snow, the buildings low in the distance, and the sounds of the street fade as we move further into the park.

Something I figured out quickly, if someone hasn't been to Central Park, it doesn't matter. Thanks to all the New York movies we've watched, the park is imprinted in our memories. The stones, the light posts, the arches of the footbridges, a person has already seen it all even if they never have. I'm one of those people. I feel at home in a place I've never been.

Still following Marilyn, we make our way, passing couples, tourists, singles hunched in coats with scarves high around their necks, and a couple dog walkers trotting behind pooches in slickers. Some people nod at our caroling. Some ignore us. Some join in as they pass by.

When I spot the first of the dancing elves, I have no idea they are waiting for us. There are three of them, each is wearing a green velvet suit jacket and yellow pants. Behind them are about a dozen people wearing white body suits. As if that isn't enough, their body suits are covered in twinkling lights. Then I see the dancers wearing mini-Santa suits, like the Rockettes wear.

Marilyn jogs forward, yelling, "Fabulous Festive Flashmob!" She holds her phone up, pauses, then shouts, "Hit it!"

The elves stride forward, the one in the center begins singing *All I Want for Christmas is You.* The other two elves join in, bells jingle from their wrists. Their beautiful *a cappella* style floats through the frosty air. Next the twinkling dancers, arms swaying, weave their voices into the mix, adding a layered background of chorus and jazzy rap sounds. The tiny lights skim through the night, leaving trails like shooting stars. The front elf steps to the side, so the mini-Santas can burst through the center, gyrating and shimmying, shaking their hips and smiling their red-lipsticked smiles. Oh wait, as they get closer, I realize they aren't mini-Santas at all. Some of them are over six feet. It's just the dresses that are small. Smallish.

Holy crap, I'm not filming.

I scramble to get a live feed going, then skip around the get different angles.

Next, alternately sashaying and strutting, the elves and twinkling dancers sing *Walking in a Winter Wonderland.*

Shakira steps over to talk quietly in my ear. "Tag Juilliard, Columbia, and NYU in your posts."

By the time they reach the end of their last song, *Rockin Around the Christmas Tree,* we're surrounded by a crowd of bystanders, many of them singing along. At the end, the performers erupt in a round of hugs for Marilyn, then dive for the blankets they've stashed behind a bench. The crowd applauds, then disperses, and soon we're waving goodbye to the Fabulous Festive Flashmob who is now huddled under their blankets and headed out of the park.

Tom and Shakira round us up and guide us back through the tree-lit walks, back toward the street. One of the most amazing days of my life is just about over. But I'm okay with that because who knows what tomorrow holds?

Chapter Ten

I get an answer to that question at 11:30 the next morning.

The five of us are again seated at the conference table. This time, we're watching the street below where shoppers and the business crowd headed to lunch are mixing together in a flurry of color. The snow has let up, and the sun is out, so it's a great time to get some different street shots.

Tom and Shakira come in together, nearly shining with glee. I can't tell who is more excited about this contest—us or them.

"Ready for today's challenge?" Shakira asks from the doorway.

Marilyn is the first to reply. "You know it."

Carl nods slowly and Flynn, Nula and I wait quietly.

"We're going to send you out, one at a time."

Tom holds up five envelopes. "Each of you have a different treasure hunt list. Find each item or person on the list, do a post about it or with it."

"Be back here by 5:00." Shakira takes the envelopes from Tom, shuffles them, then hands each of us one.

"There are two other rules," Tom adds. "One, don't open your envelope until you're out on the street. Two, no communicating with each other or anyone else from MLNY, until 5:00 tonight."

Shakira hands me my envelope, then stands back to talk to all of us. "That includes looking at each other's feeds."

Tom says, "Honor system on both of those. We trust you all."

Envelope in hand. Flynn stands. "I'm number one? I go first?"

As soon as Tom nods, Flynn is out the door.

"We'll wait five minutes between exits." Shakira slides into a chair. "That'll give enough time for the elevator."

My envelope is number five, so I sit back to enjoy the view.

Twenty minutes later, I'm finally in the elevator, clutching my envelope and staring at the glowing numbers, waiting to descend. The classical Christmas music is floating down from the speaker. When the car slows, my heart does a little jump. Sure enough, the car halts at five, the doors glide open, and there is Ethan. Today he's wearing a deep charcoal grey suit with a pale burgundy tie and looking as intimidatingly handsome as ever.

"Hello," he says.

My very original response is a simple, "Hi." The door starts to glide shut, so I reach forward to stop the motion. "Coming in?"

Why does that sound so oddly sexual?

He steps in, brushing past me because I'm still holding the door. A flash of heat blazes through me.

Once he's inside, I let go of the door and it starts gliding shut. When it's about halfway, it glitches, then stops.

Ethan reaches forward and pushes it. "Sometimes it sticks."

I don't feel so great, watching him shove the door from the side, shaking it until it starts sliding again, even though he does look kind of sexy doing it.

Once the door is again slowly gliding shut, he steps back and grins.

The car begins to descend. The four lights up, the three, then the two but then instead of the one lighting up, the whole car jerks, and stops. The light above snaps off and the Christmas music vanishes. My heart lurches as I blink into the darkness.

"Ethan?"

"Yeah. I'm here. You okay?"

I nod but then realize he can't see me. "I'm okay. Are you?"

"I am. Sorry about this."

I grab the side railing even though the car isn't moving. "It's not your fault."

"It might be." He sighs. "I knew there was a problem, but I was waiting until next week to deal with it."

"Is it just going to start working again?"

"Sort of. Once someone figures out it's stuck, they'll call the maintenance guy."

I finger the envelope as I look through the darkness at Ethan. My eyes are adjusting, and I can see his outline. Also, I can see he's looking at me. I'm smiling when I ask, "So this has happened before?"

"Once or twice." He replies, sheepishness in his voice.

I slide down to sit on the floor with my legs outstretched. The envelope in my hands.

He comes over and slides down next to me.

I feel his body even though he isn't touching me. That zing of electricity comes back and it feels great.

"I just need to—" I hear the thud of fabric as he pats his jacket. "I don't have my phone."

Instinctively, I pull mine out, tap the screen, but stop. "I'm in a contest challenge right now." And—I'm shut in an elevator with this hot guy.

"Sorry."

I'm not. Sure, I want to get out there and find whatever is on my list, but…

"One of the rules is that we aren't allowed to communicate with anyone from MLNY or any of the contestants."

There is silence, then he again says, "Sorry."

"They'll figure it out as soon as someone tries to use the elevator. Then they'll call the guy. Right?"

He waits, then sighs again, then replies. "I suppose so."

There is a beat of silence as we settle into our situation. I start to think about the last time we were in this elevator. I wonder if he is too.

"You sure you're okay with this?" He asks, softly. "How long do you have for your challenge?"

"Until 5:00." And I was more than fine with giving up a few minutes to sit side by side with him. "It's not so bad." I tip sideways and bump him with my shoulder. "You're here." After a pause, I add, "I don't think this counts as contacting you."

He bumps me back. "It's my fault the elevator isn't fixed."

I drop my phone into my bag. "You can't run everything."

"You're the only one who seems to think that."

I tuck the envelope in the bag. "Your brothers and sisters?"

He doesn't say anything, so I continue. "They depend on you."

"I want them to depend on me."

"But you need to have a life too." I think about what he told me during dinner. "You were there when they needed you. They're grown adults now. It's time…"

"What?" He taps my leg. "Time for what?"

"This is going to sound pretty strange," I stop, but something about Ethan makes me continue. "I don't know why, but I started thinking about my dad."

"That's why you stopped talking?"

"No, I don't think so. I stopped because I started thinking about my dad."

"You miss him?"

"I do, but that isn't it."

"What were you going to say. About time?"

"It's time for you to be you. You know, to have your own life instead a life that's about taking care of other people."

"That made you think of your dad? Maybe you think it's time for him to do the same thing."

I do. I just didn't know that I did. I nod, then add. "I guess so."

"Makes sense." I like the way he says it. Calm and thoughtful. No wonder his siblings trust him and depend on him.

We're quiet again until I bump him again. "Is this what people do in stalled elevators? Have deep conversations?"

I feel him shift, then reach across me to touch my cheek with his fingertips, turning my face toward him. "I like talking with you."

"I like talking with you too."

72

"Thanks."

"Okay if I kiss you?"

I'm nervous and excited. "I didn't ask before I kissed you."

He speaks softly. "I can't see your face."

I arch forward, tension gripping my spine, making me needy. He leans forward. Our lips touch. I sag into him.

His arm goes around my back, and he deepens the kiss. His scent surrounds me. The taste of him ignites me. I reach for him, slide my hand inside his jacket and feel the hard muscles beneath his soft dress shirt. It's absolute fiery heaven kissing him.

He tightens his grip on me, then leans back, lifting me off the floor, closer to him.

I feel myself heating up, melting, and I can't take my mouth off his. I start to crawl onto him, needing to get closer.

The car jolts. The light blinks on. The tinny classical Christmas music drifts down from above. Seconds later, the doors glide open.

Chapter Eleven

Late Wednesday afternoon, Ethan stood outside Carlson's school, watching the front door of the building for his nephew. The mid-week pickup after Carlson's chess club was one of his favorite duties as uncle. They'd head to his apartment, make dinner, and hang out until his sister Beatrice came to collect Carlson.

The sun was already low on the horizon, and the sky was filled with thick grey clouds. The weather reports were calling for heavy snow, starting first thing tomorrow morning and lasting all day. If the city got as much as the report indicated, it was going to be the heaviest snow fall so far that winter. Perfect for the last few days before Christmas.

The school door swung open then a pair of girls burst through, taking the concrete steps two at a time as they raced to the sidewalk. Just when the door was about the swing closed, Carlson came through. With his plaid scarf, grey duffel coat and canvas shoulder bag, he looked like a miniature version of one of the thousands of college students that mingled throughout the city.

He marched down the steps and came to a stop. "Afternoon, Uncle E. I did not win all the matches, but I played well enough."

Together, they turned and started the walk uptown.

The usual traffic rumbled beside them, a mix of cars, honking taxis, and diesel engine trucks.

"Aside from that, how is your academic career progressing this week?" The question about school netted him a detailed list of studies examined in science, works discussed in English class, and an overall assessment of end of semester assignments. Throughout it all, Ethan did his best to pay attention, but it was difficult. It wasn't that Carlson's update was uninteresting. Ethan had been having trouble concentrating on his own thoughts ever since he and Emma had tumbled out of the elevator. Well, any thoughts that didn't include that kiss and what could've happened if the maintenance guy hadn't shown up when he did.

"Tomorrow's your last day at the office, right?"

A twinge of guilt pinched Ethan. Apparently, he'd been talking shop too often with his nephew. He made a mental note to lighten up. "Don't you have better things to think about?"

Carlson turned his hands up. "It's the last day of school until after New Year's."

"Yes, it is the last full workday." Tomorrow was also going to be his last chance to see Emma. Late in the afternoon, he'd clean out his office, take it down to the bare minimum, then slip out after everyone was gone for the day. First thing Friday, in the staff meeting, he'd share his own news with the staff. He's be officially done by 8:30. He wasn't worried about putting himself on silent mode. He was beginning to worry about what he was going to do with himself. This would be the first time in his entire life that his schedule wouldn't be filled with responsibilities for work and others.

They rounded a woman adjusting shopping bags

hanging from her dog stroller. Carlson paused to say hello to the Chihuahua and compliment it on the green Christmas sweater it was sporting. Ethan smiled. Dogs wore sweaters, so why not chickens wearing sweaters?

Carlson scurried to catch up to Ethan. "Did you pick a girlfriend yet?"

Ethan shrugged. Again, he wondered, why had he let himself be talked into setting up that account? The women were attractive. They were probably interesting too. None of them could be anything like Emma. She was one of a kind. She was also about to walk out of his life.

"Mom says you should have one in time for the family Christmas dinner. If you don't have a date the table will be off. Odd numbers aren't right at dinners. Apparently."

"Your mom doesn't think these random women have families of their own to eat with on Christmas?" The idea that these women didn't have friends or families to spend the holiday with was so wrong he wouldn't even entertain the notion. He also didn't want to think about sitting beside some random stranger, no matter how beautiful.

"I don't know what's my mom is thinking."

They turned the corner and the door to his building was in sight. "If I delete the app, will that delete my account as well?"

"You're supposed to be using it, Uncle E." Carlson stopped short and looked up at him with earnest eyes. "To get a girlfriend."

"What's it to you?" Ethan stopped and slipped his hands into his pockets.

"Inspiration." His nephew stared at the ground, kicked at nothing, then tugged on his shoulder strap. "If you can get one, it'll give me hope. Maybe I can get one. You know. When I'm older."

This was turning in to one of those emotional moments uncles are supposed to have with their nephews. He had to say the right thing, but all he had was the truth. "I don't think using an app is the way to get an actual girlfriend."

Carlson cast him a quizzical glance. "What other way is there?"

Elevators. "Real life."

Carlson sighed and started walking again. "I don't think deleting the app will get rid of your account. I don't think so, but I don't know for certain."

Relieved, Ethan started walking too. "Glad we reached the limit of your knowledge."

"Me too." Carlson eyed him over his shoulder. "But I still expect you to get a girlfriend."

***

Thursday at about 6:30, Ethan was nearly done packing up his office. The storm had come as predicted and outside on the street below, trucks and cars rolled slowly through the thick, wet snow already heaped across the roads. Snow was piled on top of awnings, light posts, rooftops and every non-moving surface.

Two small boxes shouldn't be enough to hold all his personal possession, but it was. He'd tossed out all the trade show nick-knacks, nametags and tote bags. He'd tidied up the binders and reference books. He'd kept the family photos, a framed drawing of the Brooklyn Bridge by Carlson, two signed Yankee baseballs and his diplomas. The office was down to bare essentials, functional for the occasional times he planned to come in, but nothing to give it a personal flare. The two boxes on the floor by the chair mocked him. Apparently, there hadn't been much personal there in the first place. Fine. Just another confirmation that he was doing the right thing. He was about to tape the boxes shut when he realized he'd left his notebook on the conference table.

He checked the hall to be sure no one was around to ask him why he was packing up his office, then headed to the elevator. The door slid open, and the Christmas music welcomed him when he stepped inside. The music was nice, but kind of slow and traditional. Not the upbeat sound that someone might expect from an ad agency. He had approved that song list. It was probably the same Christmas music they'd been playing since his mom and dad were there.

The elevator rose smoothly, and the doors opened without a glitch. The hall upstairs was as quiet as the one on his floor. He rushed past the empty reception desk, striding quickly to the conference room.

He stopped short in the doorway. The big room wasn't empty as he'd expected. There was a woman standing in front of the window, her phone raised to capture both her face and the neon lit snowstorm outside. Alerting her to his presence would have been the gentlemanly thing to do, but he didn't do that. Instead, he watched her graceful motions and the play of expressions passing over her face. The lights from the street moved across her, brightening the side close to him while casting a shadow over her opposite shoulder.

After a moment she spotted him, stopped, and lowered her phone.

"Sorry," he said, wishing she hadn't stopped. "I didn't mean to interrupt you."

She came away from the window, everything about

her movements telling him she was embarrassed about being caught taking selfies.

"Get some nice ones for your followers?" he asked.

She set her phone on the table next to her laptop bag. "I guess so."

He looked from the snowy cityscape behind her to her face, still illuminated by the lights from the street and buildings. "I bet you did."

"Thanks." Her reply was soft, hesitant. She touched the hem of her midnight blue cocktail dress. "They took us out to dinner. You know, our last night here…"

He didn't want to think about that. "Are the pictures for some part of today's contest challenge?"

"Nope. Today's challenge was a video chain letter. We had to tag someone we'd met here in the city in a video post and get them to repost it."

Unsure of what any of that meant, he just nodded.

"I'm guessing the goal was to see how far the posts would go."

Again, he just nodded.

"I tagged Sammi."

"And he reposted it?"

"He sure did. He spliced the video into three sections and reposted each with dozens of tags. His chickens are famous now, and I have more followers."

She seemed happy enough when she said it, but her smile didn't quite reach her eyes.

Who could blame her? There were questions between them. There was also the undeniable connection. A connection, it seemed, he could do nothing about. A connection that was going to be broken tomorrow. "Have your followers been asking about your chickens back home?"

Even with the distance between them, she saw the smile light up her eyes. "Yes, actually, they have." She turned toward him and leaned her hip against the conference table. "My dad has been sending me photos to post, but, well…"

"He isn't as good as you are?"

"He does his best, but chickens are chickens, you know? They don't always want to cooperate."

He moved into the room. "I noticed that when we were at Sammi's."

She laughed.

He took a step closer. "Maybe you need to get them some sweaters. Maybe if they are cozier, they'll be more cooperative."

"New Year's sweaters with silver glitter?" she asked, her tone light, suggestive. Or was that his imagination.

He took two steps closer. "Sure. Why not." It was pretty obvious that he wasn't thinking about the chickens.

She scooted backward, seating herself on the conference table. "You think I should knit them myself?" She crossed one leg over the other and looked up at him, a challenge in her gaze. "You think that's what country people do? Knit chicken sweaters?"

"I don't know enough about what country people do. You should tell me." One more long step and he would be within an arm's length. Almost close enough to touch her.

"Why don't you come over here, closer. Maybe I'll show you instead."

He knew what he wanted. She knew what she wanted. What they both wanted. He took those last two steps and reached her.

Chapter Twelve

Since when am I this bold assertive woman who sits on conference tables and calls men over to her? Since now.

Ethan is in front of me now, and I can feel his heat, smell that fantasy inducing scent, and see the longing in his eyes. We both want this moment, more from this moment. There's no reason to back away and every reason to move forward. I set my palm on his chest, feel the soft warmth of him beneath the fabric. He's staring at me, his gaze so intense I have to look away.

I grab my phone and hop off the table. I know I'm going to go back to him, but I want to toy with him a bit first. I need this to last as long as it can because it's all I'm going to have. I glance at him then I move to the window. The night sky is a blur of white. The snow sparkles from the reflections of the city lights. I nearly plaster my face to the glass. The colors spin, and the flakes of snow seem to stretch for miles. The snowstorms at home are beautiful in their cozy, country way, but this storm is beyond that. It's wild and beautiful, intense like the city, bigger than itself, brought to life by the lights, traffic, and the people determined to get to wherever they are headed despite the storm. At home, people rush out to buy milk and bread then head home to stay put. This city doesn't stop.

"I've never seen anything like it." I say it with a sigh,

realizing I'll miss the intensity, the vividness, the constant challenge.

He comes up behind me, and I feel the heat from his body. The scent of his aftershave, familiar now, makes me shiver. Twenty-four more hours, and this will all be over. I'll be home, back at the farm. Back to the life I left behind.

"Nothing like it," he replied, his deep voice soft and so close to me.

"I wish I could see where you're from. See your coop, the chickens. Meet your dad."

I laughed at the image of Ethan's shiny shoes buried in cedar shavings. "Where I'm from, there aren't any people like you."

He chuckles. "You don't think I'd fit in?"

Was it possible to be changed into a completely different person in only four days? "I don't think even I fit in."

"Do you want to?" he asked.

"No. I guess not." That was the truth. But it didn't matter. It's where I'll be. These few days have shown me that this is a big world, and I belong in it. Out here, instead of out in the middle of a cornfield.

I lift my phone and snap some pics of the dazzling swirling white. Then I made a video of the snow filled scene behind me. I show Ethan how to add *Ask Me a Question* to the Instagram story post. Then I add a vintage-style filter and add the pic to my story.

"What will they ask you?" he wants to know.

"Maybe where I am or when I'm going home. Sometimes they just send an emoji."

"How soon will they send a question?"

"Thanks to this contest, for now, right away."

He turns his attention to my phone, so I take a look. Yep. There's already a question.

Who's the hot guy next to you?

I zoom in on the photo. Sure enough, there's Ethan's reflection, floating beside me in the glass. "Look." When he leans in to look at the picture, I snap a selfie of the two of us. I post it with the caption, *Holiday Mystery Man.*

"Holiday mystery man?" He's still standing beside me, his arm brushing mine.

His voice is low and deep and makes me think about that kiss in the elevator. Thinking about what more could have happened, I nod. "That's who you are to them."

He takes the phone from me, hits the icon to turn it toward us, then leans down to kiss me as he snaps the pic. "Post that one." He lowers his voice. "I dare you."

"Dare me?" I ask in a whisper.

He nods.

I find a cute image of some mistletoe and add that along with #smoochie. I pick a filter that brightens the snow in the background and add it to my story.

"Maybe I should try harder, get past the *smoochie* stage."

I don't know what to say to that, so I just smile while my face turns red. "Are you sure no one is going to recognize you?"

He laughs. "I doubt anyone I know will see it."

"You sure about that? Nobody from here?"

"I doubt anyone from the board of directors is following your Instagram story."

"Geez." I mock frown. "I'm not sure that's a very nice thing to say."

He starts to laugh again but stops short. "Well… not them, but Shakira and Tom… probably…"

"Are." I finish for him, a smirk pulling on my mouth. "Yes, they definitely are."

He smirks too. "Yeah, I suppose they better be."

I lean in and tap his chest with my fingertips. "Do you care?"

"No." He takes my fingertips in his palm and squeeze lightly. "I'm more concerned with getting past the smoochie stage."

I like the sound of that. But it's complicated. I slide my hand out of his grip and take a few steps away. To hide my nerves, I lift my phone and snap a couple more pictures of the street below. I pick the best and add it to my story. I check my stats.

"They like the smoochie."

"What about you?" He comes to me, brushes a strand of hair off my cheek then runs his thumb down my neck.

"I liked it too."

"But?"

"But… what about the contest."

He slides his fingers around my neck. The heat from his hand spreads down my back. "Like I said before, I don't have any input. Everyone knows who the judges are—and who they aren't."

I'm having a hard time breathing and an even harder time thinking. "It still seems… complicated."

"It's not."

He moves his hand down my spine. "Trust me. There isn't going to be a problem."

No problem?

I consider that. There's only one way that he could be sure that there isn't a problem. I didn't win. I should probably be sad about that. It means that tomorrow I'll be back right where I started. But that's tomorrow. Hours away from now.

I reach up and loosen his tie. My nerves jump as my hands wrestle with the task. He must be used to sophisticated women who know all the right things to say, know all the right moves to make. Me? I'm just a country girl whose only ever had one boyfriend, such as he turned out to be. All I have is the very basic experiences with him and some ideas I've fantasized about while reading romance novels.

I tug on his tie some more. The fabric is smooth and light and feels great in my hands but, honestly, I don't know what I'm doing. It's not gliding off the way I imagined. It's starting to look a mess. I go after the knotted part, yanking and tugging until it's twisted but sort of coming off. He reaches up. In a flurry of quick motion, the tie is undone and hanging across his red striped shirt.

He loosens the top two buttons then lowers his hand to guide me back until my spine is pressed against the cool glass. Someone could be watching us through the blizzard. If they really tried, they'd be able to make out the two bodies, coming together in the fifth-floor office. Do I care? Should I care?

Now his mouth is on mine and both his arms are around my lower back. I don't care about anything except the gentle press of his mouth and the smell of his aftershave and the heavy weight of his shoulders and the very, very wonderful fact that he wants to be past the smoochie stage as badly as I do. Doing this with him will change me once and for all. I'll never be the same person I was. It won't be possible.

Whoever is on the other side of this experience, I want to meet her. Be her.

One of his hands drops lower. The other pulls me tighter to him. The cool glass sends a chill down my spine. Or maybe that's his kiss, because the kiss that started out so gentle is now turning quick and eager. I match the intensity.

I shouldn't compare this moment to the ones I had with him, the ex-boyfriend who broke apart my world, but I do. He's the only guy I'd ever really, really kissed. Hard to believe, I suppose in this day and age, but it's true. And to think I'd been planning on marrying that guy.

This moment isn't anything like those moments. My times with him had been careful, affectionate but predictable. Now I feel confident, expressive, and bold. I'm kissing Ethan as much as he's kissing me. Maybe more. Maybe I'm the one setting the pace. I like that. He likes it too.

I know that because his breathing has quickened, like me, and he's delving deeper into my mouth, his tongue caressing mine. Somewhere far off in the back of my mind, I wonder again if this is a good idea. It feels good, sure but the sensible country girl side of me keeps thinking there's something wrong with what I'm doing. For the life of me, though, I can't figure out what that might be. Or even why I'd care.

My insides are starting to quiver with taut and excited heat. Electricity sparks over my nerve endings, making my skin tingle—the places where he's touching me and everywhere else. All this excitement is making it hard for me to think. Should I be doing this? Where is it going?

If I was making out with a guy back home, I'd know for sure he'd tell someone, or everyone, about it tomorrow. Then there would be a public assessment of my behavior. Ethan's not going to tell anyone. How do I know? I just do. It's just me and him, getting hot and bothered together. Consensually. All adult like.

I keep kissing him. I slide my hands up under the heavy fabric of his jacket, my palms gliding over his shirt, feeling the heat of his body. I have to lean to the side to give my arms space to drop lower. I move my arms around his waist, and I'm close to him again. He's not that much taller than I am, so my breasts are pressed into his chest, my hips near his. My body's getting hotter and I want to touch more of him. All of him.

I set aside the last of my musings and decide I'm all in. Wherever it is that we're headed, I'm going.

* * *

If he wanted to, Ethan could blame his impulsive behavior on the season. The festive decorations, the excited mood of his staff and family, the silly Christmas songs. Too much frosting. Too many red and green sprinkles. The bright lights strung around pillars covering entire buildings, blinking at him from everywhere, made him dizzy and disoriented.

Don't forget the mistletoe.

But of course, that was all a load of justified crap.

He wanted Emma, and he wanted her bad. He wanted more than these kisses. He wanted more than just random meet-ups. Gradually, he slowed the pace until he could pull back enough to talk. His breathing was quick, his heart thumping against her. "You're leaving tomorrow."

She stilled but didn't pull back. "Yeah, I am."

Whatever they did tonight wasn't going to be enough. He wanted more than a memory with her. He wanted her. "We—" *won't see each other again.* He couldn't get the words out. Was she thinking them too?

"We can." She smiled at him, her lips puffy and moist from their kisses.

"We can…?"

"Do this." Eyes bright, she tipped her head down, looking at their bodies pressed together. "I want to."

Chapter Thirteen

His hands rested on the small of her back. She felt right in his arms, standing there with him, the darkened, snowy, city skyline stretching out behind her. "Your hair is glowing."

She lifted an eyebrow, half smiling. The other half of her expression was telling him to stop talking and start kissing her again.

He scanned the horizon stretched out behind her. Two building were completely covered in tiny white lights. One had a row of red and green neon wreaths. A sheen of color illuminated the outline of her hair. "From the lights," he added, wanting to clarify.

She pulled her lips together and rolled her eyes upward. "Like I have a halo?"

It was his turn to half smile. "Exactly like that."

Now she was looking straight at him. "I'm not an angel, though."

And he was looking straight at her. "I'm not so sure about that."

"Are you going to stop talking now?" She tapped his calf with her foot. "Give me a chance to prove it?"

He didn't need any more invitation than that. He leaned into her, took her hands in his and lifted her arms wide, like a snow angel. But instead of swinging them up and down, he laced his fingers between hers, then locked her hands against the windowpane, holding her arms wide, so he could concentrate on kissing her, tasting her, and feeling her body beneath his.

At first, she strained against him, but soon she softened and let him set the pace. Once her mouth was well used, he moved down to run a strand of kisses down her neck then across her collarbones. Once he got to the top swell of her breasts, he lowered their hands. Reluctantly, he unlaced his fingers. The loss of connection was fleeting, because soon he had unzipped the back of her dress. She shimmied. The dress fell.

He took one breast in each hand. She sighed and closed her eyes, accepting his touch, accepting the sensual pleasure he offered. The warmth filled his palms. Her breath warmed his neck. Her breathing turned raspy, her movements a combination of restlessness and fluid stillness.

He dropped down to take one of her nipples in his mouth. It tightened. She groaned. He ran his tongue across it, sucked it deeper into his mouth, and felt her whole body respond. He took his time, tasting her skin then moving to the other breast to give it the same attention as the first. She murmured her appreciation, her hands in his hair, her fingers skimming over his scalp, caressing his neck.

He dropped to his knees, then moved one hand to slide it over her stomach. The smooth skin under his fingertips was warm and soft. He moved his hand lower, ran his index finger under the band of her panties.

She put her hand over his, stopping him from tugging them lower. "Wait."

She shoved her hands under his jacket, pushing it off

his shoulders. Once it was on the floor, she started on the buttons of his shirt. He worked with her, then twisted out of it, and then yanked the undershirt off, threw it to the floor on top of the shirt. Then he felt her moving, sliding down the window, lowering herself to her knees. Now her hands were on his bare skin, her fingers gliding over him, pausing, moving, then pausing again.

She glanced up at him. "I want to remember what you look like."

Her words made him shiver. "I want to remember you too," he said, lowering himself to the floor. She looked from his mouth to his eyes, then leaned over to press her mouth to his, clearing his mind of everything except the need to touch and taste her.

When she reached for his belt, he helped her loosen the buckle. Together, they undid the button, then lowered his zipper. Seconds, later, the last of their clothes were scattered across the conference floor.

Chapter Fourteen

Friday morning at about 9:30, I make my way to the conference room. Even though Monday morning was only four days ago, it might as well have been a lifetime. I may look the same, and sound the same, but I'm not the same. Sure, I'm headed home to the life I left behind, but that's okay. I'm not the same and that will make everything different. At least I hope it will.

I think it will.

Maybe it will.

It will.

Definitely. I think so.

I pause outside the door, watching the other finalists mill around the coffee table. Marilyn and Carl are side by side, their heads low as Nula scrolls through her phone, probably showing them her stunning Instagram feed. I'd checked it out this morning. It's a collection of selfies she's taken over the week. She must've posed next to five different Santas and 12 different decorated trees. And that was just on her feed. Cannabis Carl and Marilyn had been busy too. Apparently, they'd spent the time after dinner last night taking each other's pictures. Flynn's feed was a stream of him in different fitness centers. Who knew one city could have so many CrossFit gyms?

I'm happy to see them, my temporary best friends,

excited about their week in the city and anxious to find out who is the contest winner.

"Excuse me, do I have frosting on my face?"

It's Carlson, Ethan's nephew. "You do." I point to his right cheek.

He holds the cookie up and inspects it. "You'd think if I can make dozens and dozens and never get any on me, I could manage to eat one and stay clean."

"You made these?" Now that he said it, given the loads of sprinkles, it made sense. I look over the tray and pick up one of the yellow-frosted stars coated with silver sprinkles.

"I did." He's looking at me now, nodding. "Uncle E helped me."

Ethan, wearing a starched white apron, a rolling pin in one hand and a bag of flour in the other. Made sense given what he'd told me about how things were when he was growing up. "He bakes with you?"

"No." Carlson wiped some but not all the yellow frosting off his cheek. "Mostly he does email and talks to me while I make them."

"That's helpful too." I take a bite. The crushing of the sprinkles makes my head vibrate.

"It is. I don't mind that he's multi-tasking. I just wish he'd focus more."

I swallow and move to the bowl of spiced eggnog. "Seems to me he works pretty hard."

"He does focus on work. That's not what I mean." He wipes off most of the rest of the frosting. "I mean focus on the app."

I lift the handle of the long dipper. "He's designing an app?"

"No, the dating app. He's trying to find a girlfriend."

93

The handle of the eggnog server clatters against the bowl. Hand shaking, I reach for it and try to serve myself some eggnog. "Oh, that's… that's… nice."

"I guess so." He pops the last piece of his cookie into his mouth, grabs another from the platter, waves goodbye, then wanders over to the tree and begins adjusting the ornaments.

There's nothing wrong with Ethan using dating apps. I'm probably the only single person on the planet that doesn't have some sort of online dating profile. It doesn't mean anything. It's not like Ethan and I had any kind of commitment.

I watch Carlson straighten some of the lights. Flynn comes up beside him and starts to help, adjusting the ones up higher. I can tell the two of them are talking as they work.

At the back of the room, Tom is starting to wave people over to the conference table. There are place cards for each of us, arranged in alphabetical order. I take my place by mine, between Marilyn and Nula. Flynn and Carl are at the end.

Shakira gets up to talk, and I keep my face forward and pleasant as she thanks us all for entering the contest and says all the things one would expect her to say at that moment. I really am trying to pay attention, but the image of Ethan, scrolling through dozens of beautiful city-polished women keeps drifting through my mind. It's making me queasy and confused. Neither of those reactions make sense. I want to regret what I've done with him, but I don't. I think that probably I should regret it, but again, I don't.

All of a sudden, everyone is applauding. Flynn is smacking Marilyn. She holds her hand up for a high five.

After he smacks her palm, she rises, opens her arms wide, and grins. Everyone is clapping, and she is awe-inspiring as she soaks up the win.

I raise my fist for a bump, and she gives it a small punch which she follows with the slow-mo finger open for the explosion. She's totally beaming, and everyone is applauding. Tom and Shakira come over, guide her to the front of the room, and the photographer is back, snapping pictures of the three of them. It makes sense. Her social media is totally different from ours, and she has done the one thing none of us has done. She has the most diverse group of followers.

I'm excited for Marilyn. Really, I am. The announcement of the winner means this is really over. It's almost time for me to head to the airport.

There's no sign of Ethan. That makes sense too, because he doesn't have anything to do with this contest. There's no reason for him to be here. I need to stop expecting him to show up.

I hang around for the rest of the after party. After hugging Marilyn and making sure we have each other's contact information, and saying goodbye to everyone else, I gather my stuff and start down the hall.

"Emma, wait. We'd like to talk to you." It's Tom calling to me.

Shakira is behind him, her bell bracelet jingling as she waves over his head. "Meet us down on the fifth floor. In Ethan's office. Ten minutes?"

My shoulders stiffen. "Um, sure." I don't want to. I really don't want to. But flat out saying no seems unprofessional and stupid. Also, not nice. Nodding, I step toward the elevator and push the button. "I'll head down now."

They've both started to back away. Tom calls to me again. "Perfect. Ethan's office is the one at the end of the hall. It looks almost empty. We just need to make sure everyone is all set up here."

Shakira's bracelet jangles again as she waves. Then she pivots and marches purposely down the hall.

Beside me, the elevator doors glide open. Heart heavy, I step in and push the five.

Because everyone is at the party upstairs, the lobby is quiet. I glance at the mistletoe archway as I pass through. Steps slowing, I move down the hall. The other doors are closed, so figuring out which office is Ethan's is easy. I pause in the doorway and study the room. Except for the wide monitor, the desk is bare. The shelves hold black binders and a few thick books. There aren't any pictures, pieces of art, or anything that reflect a human works in the room. Seems odd, considering how involved he is with his family. I move deeper into the room, all the way to the window. The view is the same as the conference room. There is a white note pad on the desk. A pen lies beside it. My fingers twitch. I could leave him a note. What would I write?

Thanks for the hot time. Bye.

Ugh. I just want this to be over. I paste on a relaxed expression and sit in the chair at the round table by the wall.

Breathe in. Breathe out. And I wait. I feel like a kid in the principal's office.

Shakira's bells jangle in the distance, getting louder as she and Tom come down the hall.

Breathe in. Breathe out. How much do they know? They must know something. Why else would they want to talk to me? So what if I messed around with Ethan. He had nothing to do with the contest.

Still, I'm embarrassed, and I feel like a jerk. But what about Ethan? It's not like I acted alone. Tom and Shakira pass through the door, then bustle into the room. They sit, one on each side of me, and pivot so they're both staring right at me.

"Thanks for staying to talk to us," Shakira says.

There's an odd smile on her mouth. Tom is smiling too. Honestly, they both look a bit odd. They don't look like they're about to chew me out.

"Do you know why you didn't win the contest?" Tom asks.

Because someone told you what kind of person I really am? Because you saw the smoochie post?

I don't say those things. I say, "I appreciate being a finalist. Marilyn is awesome. You picked the right person."

"She is amazing," Shakira says.

Tom adds, "We're excited about what she's doing."

I nod. Maybe they're having this talk with the other four finalists too. I don't know what to say.

"We're excited about what you're doing, too."

"Oh. Thanks." I still don't know what to say.

"You still don't know why we want to talk to you?"

I shake my head.

"We want to offer you a job."

Chapter Fifteen

Monday morning after feeding the girls, I make myself a to-go coffee, then climb into my Jeep to drive to the hospice. The same wreath is hanging on the door. Inside, there's a woman behind the welcome desk wearing a pair of deer antlers. Singing along to *Frosty the Snowman*. The same potted poinsettias circle the reception area. Seeing them there makes me realize how much I've experienced since last time I stood in that exact same spot.

Granna is expecting me, so after I stop at the front desk, she appears within a couple minutes. Sporting a bright red sweater and green track pants, she comes straight up to me and does her best to pull me into a hug. I wrap my arms around her and squeeze very gently.

Slowly, I ease her back then take her elbow. Together we walk to the lounge area and find a table near the window. It's more crowded than last time. The chatter is a constant buzz around us.

Once we're settled, she reaches across the table and takes my hands in hers. "Tell me everything about your trip."

"Like I said when I called. I didn't win."

"So what? You went all the way to New York City. I know something wonderful happened. I can see it on your face."

Yeah. Something wonderful did happen. But then it didn't. "There's something I want to tell you."

Her gaze is soft, curious, but not impatient.

Telling her is the right thing to do. Speaking softly, I say, "We aren't together anymore."

"I know." Her gaze stays steady. "I was hoping he'd tell me himself, but I understand why he doesn't." She shrugs then pats the back of my hand. "Are you going to tell me about New York now?"

"Of course." My smile is genuine but fades.

After she releases me, she pats my shoulder and says, "Wait just a minute before you start." She reaches into the pocket of her track pants and pulls out that tiny spiral notebook. She flips through until she finds the page she's looking for. I see now that it has my name at the top and some notes about the contest and the dates I went to the city. She uncaps the pen that had been slipped into the wire spiral. "Now, I'm ready."

I tell her all the best parts: the fun I had doing my presentation on the first day, meeting Sammi and seeing the adorable chicken sweaters he'd knitted, the amazing holiday New York Christmas decorations, and about meeting the other contestants. I leave out the kiss, me falling for Ethan, and having crazy-wild, hot sex with him in his conference room.

While I talk, she jots down a few notes. After I tell her about how the chickens were fine Friday night when I returned, she closes the notebook and pushes it back into her pocket. "Come see my suite. It has a view of the woods."

I help her up, then take her elbow.

Arm in arm, the two of us walk slowly through the halls, stopping to be introduced to the people she's become friendly with. Everyone is great, as great as they can be considering, and soon we're admiring that view in her suite. The trees out back are mostly bare. A few have branches with hardy leaves still clinging to them. The dots of yellow and red are especially bright against the faded brown and grey trunks. Beyond the hardwoods are pines and firs.

"I bet it looks amazing when it snows," I say.

When I turn around, I see that Granna is stretched out across the bed, her thin legs still under the light throw pulled over them. I go to her and bend down to hug her lightly. "Thanks again for entering me in that contest. You're right, I never would've done that myself."

"I can't wait to hear what happens next."

My stomach knots. It's okay that's she's forgotten that I didn't win and that nothing will be happening next.

"Thank you for coming." She takes her glasses from around her neck and sets them on the bedside table in front of a couple framed photographs. One of the pictures is of him and me. It was taken the night we went to senior prom. I'm wearing a yellow beaded gown I bought at a resale shop. The bliss on my face makes me sad. I look away.

"I hope you don't mind," she says touching my arm. "I love you both, and it's the only picture I have to remember you both by."

"It's beautiful," I say. And I mean it.

* * *

Tuesday night as I clear the dishes from the dining room table, my dad brings the box of tree ornaments up from the basement. With my mom gone, it's tough to get excited about putting up the tree. With only three days until Christmas we can't put it off any longer. He sets the box down, then his hands to tell me that Kenny came by and asked about the chickens.

Kenny is a kid who lives down the street. Even though he's five years younger than me, I know him from school. We rode the bus together. Sometimes he'd get off at my house and helps me with the birds. Then walks home. Now we stay in touch through Instagram. He must've known I was in the city, that I'd left the girls behind in the care of my dad.

What about them, I ask.

How they are doing?

I don't want to admit it to myself, but I feel kind of guilty. I've been off, using the girls to make myself look good, and they've been back here without me. Some committed chicken farmer I am.

I help my dad open the lid. Together we lift out the individual boxes still labeled in my mom's neat printing.

Once the top is off, I ask, *Everything was ok? With the chickens?*

He nods and offers a thumbs up . *I think he wants to know if you need help*, he adds.

It's my turn to nod and offer a thumbs up.

Do you? He's looking at me now, intently.

I shake my head.

You have something to tell me. He sits on the couch and pats the spot next to him. *There's something I need to tell you, too.*

I sit. *Who first?*

He reaches into his grey Dickies and pulls out a quarter. He sets it on his knee. *Heads or tails?*

My reply, *heads.*

The coin goes up. He snatches it out of the air, then smacks it onto his wrist. Tails.

He slips the coin back into his pocket. *I want to sell the farm.*

Wow. Holy crap. What the hell. I'm happy. I'm sad. I'm stunned. Then all at once I realize, it's the right thing for him to do. I want to tell him I'm glad but all I manage is *okay*.

It's okay? he asks, then puts his hand on mine.

Yes. I understand. Where will you go?

He takes his hand off mine. *Taos, to see my brother. Stay with him a while. Then…* He shrugs.

I grab him into a hug, hold on to him, long enough to feel him breathe. He knows I understand. Living here without my mom, it's been hard for me. For him, it must be misery. His back eases, and I feel him soften with a sigh. I hold him a bit longer, tears pressing against my eyelids. Happy tears? Happy for him, knowing he's doing what's right. Doing what he needs to.

Finally, he gives me one last squeeze and lets out one last breath. I let go at the same time he does.

He waits until I'm looking, then signs. *Not until this summer. Okay? It'll take time. What about you?* I know it's my turn. I already let him know I had something to tell him, so there's no getting out if it. He's looking at me now, his eyes damp, his focus intense.

My heart is thumping, my hands quivering. Just as he did, I dive in. *They offered me a job.*

Still looking at me, he nods. He's smiling. Where is his shock? Surprise?

I tell him again. *They offered me a job. In New York. That's wonderful. When do you start?*

I haven't accepted it yet. I told them I wasn't sure.

He's frowning.

I can't tell him the whole story. I can't tell him why I'm not taking the job. I just want him to know I'll be okay. Now I have the other thing. I lift my hands, wanting to tell him, but it's so much harder now that I'm in front of him.

Go ahead, he tells me.

I want to tell him the rest. That I met someone who made me forget all about the past. Someone who showed me that I have a future.

But my hands don't move. Instead I shake my head. *That's all, really.*

I can tell he doesn't believe me, but patient as always, he doesn't push.

Chapter Sixteen

Wednesday morning, the day before Christmas Eve, I step off the porch, phone in my pocket, coat zipped all the way up. There is no snow, so the ground is grey with frost and hard from the cold. Puffs of air float in front of my face. The only sound is the thud of my boots hitting the ground. The smoke from my dad's wood burner drifts up into the dawn. He didn't used to drink his morning coffee out in the barn, alone except for the cows. I get it now. He comes out here to avoid being in bed without my mom. To avoid drinking his morning coffee alone. Him selling the farm and moving is the right thing. For sure.

I reach the coop and unlatch the door. What will happen to me? The girls? The latch rattles breaking the quiet.

That's a problem for another day. I step in, smell the wood shavings and the sweet musky scent of the chickens. It's dim and silent.

Louisa, nestled in one of the boxes, coos. One of the other birds cackles softly. Cluck Norris, perched in the corner on the cross bar, is sound asleep. His beady little eyes squeezed shut. His attitude unnoticeable for now. I push the door closed and begin checking the scene. I like to make sure it's tidy and cute in the coop before I decide where and how to start the Insta feed. I straighten one of the chains for the hanging feeder and pick some shavings out of the water. The girls stay in their boxes, eyeing me sleepily.

I'm early. There are still several minutes before the sun slices up over the horizon.

I slip my phone onto the new selfie stick, make sure the flash is off, then take a couple pics. I can use a filter later, see if I can get them to lighten up enough for use. Once a have a couple that will probably work, I pause to think over what I'm going to say. Some sort of Merry Christmas message is in order. I haven't been live since I came back from the city. I'd already made it public that I hadn't won and received dozens and dozens of encouraging messages. Sales are up, likes and engagements are up. Things are good.

Sort of.

The first rays of lights skim over the fields, making the snow pink. I need to decide what to say. I need to get a smile on my face. "Louisa? Any ideas about what we should say this morning?"

She stares blankly at me as I continue talking. "Other than 'Hey, we're cute. Buy some more stuff'?"

"How about Merry Christmas?"

That voice. Chills run down my spine. My throat tightens.

"Or are you more of a Happy Holidays type small business owner?"

I turn to see him in the doorway. His camel coat is buttoned all the way up. A red and green plaid scarf is wrapped around his neck. "I say both. And Happy Hanukkah—if it is Hanukkah."

"Boxing Day?" he asks, taking a step forward.

My heart lurches. "Sure. Canada is right over the bridge."

He steps all the way in, then pushes the door closed. His shoes are already covered by chicken-messed cedar shavings.

I point my selfie stick at him. "Want to tell me what you're doing here? In my chicken coop?"

The hens are starting to rustle in their boxes. One pops out and hops over to peck at Ethan's laces.

He watches the bird, unconcerned, then gestures to my phone. "It's Wednesday morning. Time for the sunrise session with the girls. I knew you wouldn't be inside your house."

I pull the selfie stick back and cross my arms. "Since when do you pay attention to Instagram?"

He begins to unwrap the festive scarf. I can't stop watching his hands. "I don't pay attention to Instagram. I pay attention to you."

"You don't need to do that," I reply as I try to deny the rush of blood heating my entire body.

"I think I do," He pulls the scarf the rest of the way off. "I think I should have from the start."

"You don't have to feel guilty about what happened. I was the one who kissed you."

"I don't think you understand what I'm saying." He takes a step forward.

"Look." I take a step back. "I kissed you. I had sex with you."

Louisa hops from her box, joins the other hen pecking at Ethan's laces. Still he ignores what they're doing to his shoes and keeps his gaze on me. "So?"

I state the obvious. "You're the boss."

"And—?"

He's not listening. "Having sex to win a contest—or to get a job—is a screwed-up thing to do."

"If you're trying to say you used me, I don't believe you."

I didn't. But that's what people will think. "What difference does it make? I'm here. Back home, out in the middle of nowhere. Not your problem."

"The job offer you received was legitimate. Tom and Shakira saw the way you organized the others. The way you were willing to wait, let others go first. You have leadership skills they don't."

He did have a point. I am good at managing people. "I didn't need them to throw me a bone."

Two more hens tumble out of their boxes. Cluck Norris wakes up, but stays silent for once.

"The offer wasn't a consolation prize."

"To keep me around, so I could continue making a fool of myself. Act like some sex-starved farmgirl?"

A half smile tugs on his mouth, and I do my best to ignore it. But when he speaks, liquid heat rolls through me. "Sex-starved farmgirl?"

Despite the churning in my chest I laugh. "Yeah."

Careful not to step on the girls, he moves toward me, then loops the scarf behind my neck. "I like the sex-starved farmgirl."

I look down at his hands, still holding the ends of the scarf. The laughter stalls in my throat. "Yeah. Well. Whatever."

"Don't you need to do your live feed?"

Crap. I'd forgotten all about it. "I—I do."

"Your people are waiting." He lets go of the scarf, takes a step back. "You don't need me in here, distracting you. I'll get out of here so you can do it." He moves to the door. "Talk after?"

I nod, then lift the selfie stick and tap the screen.

107

The live feed went well. I think. Actually, I don't remember how it went. I don't remember what I said. All I could think about was the soft cashmere scarf caressing my neck and smelling like him.

Outside, Ethan is not in sight. I close the door to the coop. There's an empty car in the driveway. I head toward the house, but stop when I see that the door to the barn is ajar. My dad never leaves it open, so that only means one thing. I thrust my shoulders back, remind myself to be strong, then march to the barn.

I step through the door, pull it closed, then freeze. In the distance, I see Ethan walking alongside my dad. My dad is pointing to one of the cows and signing the cow's age. That isn't what makes me freeze. It's Ethan. He is signing back.

I rush forward, reaching them in seconds. I tap Ethan on the arm. "Why didn't you tell me you knew sign language?"

He shakes his head, as he moves his hands to say. *Ilsa.* "She taught me some. I don't know much. Yet."

"I—I…" I stand there like an idiot, looking from Ethan to my dad.

My dad grins, then walks off.

Ugh. Why does that make me so mad at him?

"Can we finish talking?" Ethan wants to know.

I take his hand and pull him to my dad's office. I shut the door, even though it isn't necessary.

"You're wrong about something," he says when I turn to him.

"Yeah. Well. Thanks. I think I figured that out already."

He sits in the battered wood chair then rests his arm on my dad's desk. "What did you figure out?"

108

"That I was wrong about why you were interested in me. I thought you understood me as a person. As a—woman."

"You were right about that," he says, calm and reasonable.

"If you understood me, about the way I am, you wouldn't have offered me a job."

" *I* didn't offer you a job."

"Yeah. You did." I'm not angry. I just want him to understand.

"No. I didn't. Tom and Shakira offered you a job. I didn't know anything about that."

"You run the place and you don't know about people getting offered jobs?" My gaze circles the office, taking in the feed store calendar, dirty work clothes hanging on the back of the door, and the piles of tool bins. "I may be a country bumpkin but even *I* don't believe that."

"I don't run the place anymore."

"They can't fire you. Your family owns it. Unless—"

"I gave the position up first thing Friday morning. Replaced myself with those two. Gave them full responsibility for all creative and management decisions."

I reach for the scarf, bury my hands in it. "You didn't know they were going to offer me a job?"

"Nope."

I take in a breath, pulling his scent deep into my lungs. "You didn't tell them to offer me a job?"

"Nope."

My voice is softer now. "You didn't say anything about me at all?"

"Nope. Well, not really." One side of his mouth lifts. "I did tell them about the chicken sweaters and about how you spoke to Ilsa."

109

I take a step forward. "I guess that's okay."

"It is. Okay."

"What about the sex?"

"What about it?"

There was no point in stalling, in being shy. "Carlson told me about the app and about how you are trying to find a date for the family Christmas party."

He gets to his feet. "I am trying to find a date for the family Christmas party."

I manage to keep from rolling my eyes. But I'm pretty sure I made a face. A not a nice one. "You're handsome and rich and, I'm guessing, well known. You won't have any problems."

He comes to me and slides his hands under the soft cashmere cuddled around my neck. "You left out that my apartment is in one of the best neighborhoods."

"Okay. Fine. Add that in." I'm trying to hold on to my mock snootiness, but it's a losing battle. He's too close, so close.

He leans into me. "If you're going to live in New York, you're going to need to understand about neighborhoods."

"Who says I'm going to live in New York?" He's close enough to kiss.

"How about you come with me to that family Christmas party? We'll talk about the move later."

"*Possible* move," I reply, leaning into him.

He pulls a sprig of mistletoe from his pocket and holds it over our heads. "I have a condition."

I look from the green twig to him. "*You*? You have a condition?"

"We bring your father. There's someone I want him to meet."

"Yes, definitely to that. But the other—it's a *possible* move."

"And this kiss?" he asks, moving his mouth to mine.

"Oh yes. Definitely, yes to that."

Isabelle Drake

Dear Santa,

Before I ran into you at Macy's, I hit up Washington Square Park again and ran into those same college kids from NYU. At least I think they were the same kids. They had that youthful energy, you know? Made me feel hip again, even if it was just for a day and a night and part of the next day. We rapped about books, life, and they showed me their phone videos. I think maybe we made one. They took me to a coffee joint where they brew stuff I can't pronounce. I stuck with my usual weed, though.

But hey, I wanted to say thanks for the smooth ride home from NYC. That sleigh of yours is epic. Beats the heck outta the bus. And the reindeer, man, those critters can fly! So high in the sky, we were. So high, all of us. Sweet time.

Until next year, keep the weed growing and the reindeer flying,

Carl

Dear Santa,

First, I'd like to let you know that this letter is from both Flynn and me. I have decided that there is more to him than his beautiful face and perfect physique, so I have taken him under my wing. He and I have drawn up a plan to increase his success by focusing on his self-control. Next year, I predict, he will be writing to you himself.
Both of us would like to say we had an exciting holiday season and enjoyed the gifts we received.

I very much appreciated the new track suits, especially the red one with the white piping. In the past, I thought red was too bright and flashy for me, but now, well, things are changing aren't they? I think next year, if you and the elves have some on hand, I'd like to try a pair of those joggers. The young people tell me you don't have to wear a matching top with these new joggers, but if it isn't too much trouble, I'd prefer to have a matching top.

My very best to you and Mrs. Claus,
Marilyn Caldwell

Isabelle Drake

Dear Santa,

I should have written last January, right after you delivered The Best Christmas Ever. So, sorry for that. Honestly, it took me a while to convince myself I wasn't on the naughty list after all. That night with Ethan, right before I moved to New York, that was pretty wild. For me, anyway.

I want to say thank you for… everything and let you know how we're all doing.

Last summer, after I moved in with Ethan, my dad took over my apartment in Greenpoint. He and Ilsa are still volunteering at the community center. I think that soon they may admit to everyone the thing we already know. They're more than 'just friends.'

My job at MLNY is exhausting, but I love it. It's the opposite of everything I ever knew growing up. Last month, I took the lead on our new client, The Feed Loft. Who better than me to create an ad campaign for feed and supplies?

I bet you want to know how things are with Ethan. He's great. He's been spending a lot of time with Carlson, who is trying to talk him in to opening a cookie bakery with the other nephews and nieces. He comes by MLNY often enough to make sure things are humming along. Other than that, there isn't much I can tell you about him that won't get me back on the naughty list.

In case you're wondering what is on my Christmas list this year, I can tell you—absolutely nothing.

With love and thanks,
Emma

P.S. Kenny from down the street adopted all my girls. If

114

you're really wanting to give me a gift, how about two dozen chicken sweaters. Order them from Sammi's Sassy Sweaters and drop them off at Kenny's farm.

Isabelle Drake

Dear Santa,

In a world filled with hashtags and double taps, Marilyn Caldwell, my partner in crime both online and offline, suggested I ditch the Instagram tags and get old-school by writing you a letter. Can you imagine? She tells me people used to do this in the 1900s. I must say, I thoroughly enjoyed selecting those adorable stickers at the mailing place she called the post office. Marilyn, my real-life friend, even helped me figure out where to slap them on the paper envelope. It's all so quaint.

Speaking of Marilyn, she told me about another holiday tradition—making a wish list for you. Now, I've got to be honest, Santa, my closets are bursting with fabulous fashion and my beauty sponsors ensure I'm always camera-ready. So, instead, I thought I'd ask for a little something to up my game. How about putting a sleek drone, a versatile green screen, and a high-quality lavalier microphone in your bag for little 'ole me?

But here's the real kicker, Santa. In the spirit of giving back to the universe, I'm including one of my latest blog posts. You'll see that I'm branching out to include travel and experience related content. Perhaps someone up there at the North Pole could use some tips to elevate their web presence! After all, even Santa's fam deserves some spotlight on the socials.

Sending you red lipstick kisses and the warmest holiday wishes,
Nula

Capturing the Magic:
Holiday Snapshot Hotspots
in the City That Never Sleeps

Well, my darlings, let's talk about these fabulous spots for holiday snapshots in the city that never sleeps!

Ice Skating at Rockefeller Center

Ah, the quintessential New York City experience! The best time to go? Twilight, my lovelies. When the city lights start to twinkle, and you're gliding on the ice, the ambiance is simply magical.

Outfit:

Channel your inner fashionista with a chic, oversized sweater, paired with black leggings and knee-high boots. Don't forget a stylish beanie and a classic red scarf for that touch of Carrie Bradshaw flair. Glide across the ice under the dazzling lights of the Rockefeller Center Christmas Tree. It's the ultimate New York City winter experience.

Best Selfie Tips:

Capture the magic with a selfie on the ice rink while twirling under the twinkling lights. Ensure great lighting by skating during the early evening. Use the rink's reflective surface for a unique angle. Hold the camera at a slightly upward angle to make the tree appear even taller in the background.

Be Tech Savvy:

Instagram: Elevate the enchanting atmosphere with filters such as Glamour or Moon.

TikTok: Add a whimsical touch using effects like Snowfall and Fairy Tale.

Stroll Through Central Park

Central Park is a year-round masterpiece, but during Christmas, it's like a winter wonderland straight out of a movie. The best time to capture its charm? Late morning, when the soft winter sunbathes the park in a warm, golden glow.

Outfit:

Embrace casual elegance with a long camel coat, a cozy turtleneck sweater, and wide-legged pants. Finish the look with ankle boots and a statement scarf. Wander through Central Park's snow-covered pathways, take a horse-drawn carriage ride, and enjoy the serene winter wonderland.

Best Selfie Tips:

Find Bow Bridge or Bethesda Terrace for picturesque backgrounds. During a snowfall, take a candid shot of yourself catching snowflakes. Use the burst mode to capture action shots of yourself and friends having a snowball fight. Experiment with black-and-white filters for a classic Central Park look.

Be Tech Savvy:

Instagram: Enhance your photos with filters like Lark or Aden for a warm, natural look that complements the park's beauty.

TikTok: Explore the classic charm of Central Park by experimenting with effects such as Nature or Vintage.

Holiday Markets at Union Square and Bryant Park

These markets are a shopper's paradise, and the best time to snap those market selfies? Early afternoon. The festive decorations and bustling crowds create the perfect backdrop for your holiday pics.

Outfit:

Layer up with a trendy faux fur-lined coat, a cable-knit sweater dress, and knee-high suede boots. Accessorize with a beret and leather gloves. Explore the festive holiday markets, sipping on hot cocoa as you shop for unique gifts and artisanal treats.

Best Selfie Tips:

Showcase your unique finds with a close-up selfie of you holding your favorite holiday market purchases. Capture the colorful market stalls in the background. For a cozy shot, hold a cup of hot cocoa with whipped cream and marshmallows. Make sure to get a bokeh effect by focusing on the festive lights.

Be Tech Savvy:

Instagram: Make the colorful market stalls pop by using filters like Juno or Lofi.

TikTok: Capture the festive spirit with effects such as Glitter or Sparkle.

Fifth Avenue Holiday Window Displays

Ladies and gents, if you want to channel your inner shopaholic and get the best shots of those glamorous window displays, go in the early evening. The dazzling lights and intricate designs are simply mesmerizing.

Outfit:

Dress to impress in a tailored black coat, a little black dress, and statement heels. Add a touch of glamour with a sparkling clutch and statement earrings. Marvel at the extravagant holiday window displays at stores like Saks Fifth Avenue and Bergdorf Goodman.

Best Selfie Tips:

Frame yourself with the extravagant window displays. Capture your reflection alongside the dazzling store decorations. Experiment with creative angles, such as reflections in mirrored surfaces. Highlight the intricate details of your outfit by using portrait mode.

Be Tech Savvy:

Instagram: Highlight the dazzling window displays with filters like Clarendon or Gingham.

TikTok: Add elegance with effects such as Glam or Lux.

The Nutcracker Ballet at Lincoln Center

A night at the ballet, dahling! For the most enchanting photos, attend the evening performance. The theater's elegance and the Nutcracker's timeless charm will leave you swooning.

Outfit:

Embrace your inner ballerina with a midi tulle skirt, a fitted sweater, and ballet flats. Don't forget a pearl necklace and delicate hairpins. Attend a performance of "The Nutcracker" at the iconic Lincoln Center and immerse yourself in the enchanting world of dance.

Best Selfie Tips:

Take a glamorous pre-show selfie in the lobby's opulent surroundings. Try to capture the grand chandeliers and the crowd's excitement in the background. After the performance, snap a selfie with the iconic Lincoln Center fountain as a backdrop. Use the theater's low lighting to your advantage.

Be Tech Savvy:

Instagram: Craft a dreamy, artistic atmosphere using filters like Amaro or Valencia.

TikTok: Enhance the ballet's ambiance with effects like Dance Party or Theater.

Christmas Eve Mass at St. Patrick's Cathedral

This is a moment of reflection and reverence. Attend the midnight mass for a truly special experience. The cathedral's grandeur is breathtaking, and the candlelit ambiance is perfect for serene photos.

Outfit:

Opt for classic elegance with a tailored black suit or a sophisticated black dress. Accessorize with a statement brooch and patent leather pumps. Attend the solemn and beautiful Christmas Eve Mass at St. Patrick's Cathedral, a cherished New York City tradition.

Best Selfie Tips:

Be discreet and respectful during the service. After Mass, take a selfie outside the cathedral with its stunning architecture in the background. Use the natural light to capture the cathedral's intricate details. Show reverence in your selfies by maintaining a solemn expression.

Be Tech Savvy:

Instagram: Enhance the cathedral's solemn beauty with filters like Mayfair or Rise.

TikTok: Add a respectful touch with Candlelight or Chapel effects.

New Year's Eve in Times Square

And finally, the pièce de résistance! For the ultimate New Year's Eve selfies, you guessed it, my dears—join the festivities at midnight. The sea of revelers, the dazzling ball drop, and the confetti showers will make your photos truly unforgettable.

121

Outfit:

Sparkle and shine in a sequined cocktail dress, statement heels, and a faux fur stole. Add a touch of drama with red lipstick. Join the crowds for the world-famous New Year's Eve celebration in Times Square, complete with the iconic ball drop and a sea of confetti.

Best Selfie Tips:

Arrive early to secure a good spot in the crowd. Take selfies with the iconic Times Square billboards as a backdrop. Capture the electric atmosphere and excitement of the countdown. Include the massive New Year's Eve ball in your selfies as it drops at midnight.

Be Tech Savvy:

Instagram: Capture the energy of the crowd with dynamic filters like X-Pro II or Ludwig.

TikTok: Add excitement to your videos with the Confetti or Fireworks effects.

So, whether you're ice skating at Rockefeller Center or attending a magical ballet performance, make sure to embrace your inner Nula and let your fashion sense shine during the festive season in New York City. After all, in the city that never sleeps, you're bound to have a truly, photo-friendly holiday experience that your followers will find unforgettable.

Remember to be considerate of others while taking selfies in these iconic locations, especially during busy holiday seasons. Now, you're ready to capture your stylish and unforgettable New York City holiday moments!

Remember to adjust the intensity of the filters to achieve the desired effect. Additionally, use Instagram and TikTok's editing tools to fine-tune your photos and videos before sharing them with your followers.

So, there you have it, a guide to the most photogenic spots during Christmas in the city. Remember, my loves, it's not just about the locations; it's about the moments and memories you capture. Until next time, keep snapping and sipping those cosmopolitans!

Dear Santa,

Namaste from the mat, my man! I trust this letter reaches you amidst your quest for enlightenment. This year, I've taken a break from my daily yoga grind to grace you with my heartfelt desires.

First things first, Santa, let's talk gratitude. I've received your gifts in the past, and while they've been okay, they've helped me keep spreading love and enlightenment through yoga. My devotees, they call themselves that, have multiplied, all thanks to your benevolence. So, yeah, thanks for the assist.

Now, about my humble requests. I'd be incredibly appreciative if you could hook me up with some swanky yoga gear. You know, top-of-the-line, eco-friendly mats that have the perfect blend of cushion and grip. And toss in some bolsters, blocks, and blankets made from organic, sustainable materials, why don't ya? Gotta keep the practice strong.

Speaking of vibes, how about some calming incense and soothing essential oils? Sandalwood, lavender, and frankincense are our jam. They're like enlightenment in a bottle, Santa. Elevate our collective meditation game, ya feel me?

In the spirit of unity and all that jazz, I'd appreciate if you could sprinkle a little extra inner peace and serenity on the world this holiday season. Your presence always brings joy, but let's kick it up a notch, shall we? Tranquility is in demand, my dude.

Now, let's get to the juicy part. I've been daydreaming about spiritual journeys, like Jamaica, man. I want to deepen my practice and share the wisdom. Hook me up with the means to make these trips happen. Picture it: the lush landscape of Jamaica, where the land's energy amplifies our spirituality. A retreat center nestled in nature, huts for our devoted followers to meditate - you know the vibe. You can just drop a deed for some sweet land in my stocking.

But hold up, there's more. I'm thinking of running a distillery on that Jamaican land. My followers can practice yoga in serene huts while we craft mindful spirits. Organic, locally sourced ingredients, man. It's all about enhancing our spiritual experiences and keeping the community flowing.

In the name of growth and all that jazz,
Flynn

P.S. Tell Marilynn Caldwell I said thanks for believing in me and my ideas. Let her know I've grown and I'm practicing self-control. Namaste!

P.P.S. If any of your North Pole elves are up for a change of scenery, they're welcome to join our New Year's Eve photo shoot in the chill huts of Jamaica. It's gonna be epic, and the vibes will be outta this world.

Dear Santa,

I trust this letter finds you in the most enchanting of spirits (or perhaps just eggnog-induced merriment?). As the holiday season gracefully draws to a close, I feel compelled to share my thoughts about someone who's become a rather interesting addition to my life: Flynn, the yoga guru. Now, before you raise an eyebrow as high as a mistletoe, let me assure you, there's more to Flynn than his knack for striking a zen pose.

Flynn has embarked on what he calls a "profound journey of self-discovery and spiritual awakening." And let's not forget his tireless efforts in spreading love and enlightenment to those lucky enough to stumble into his downward dog sessions. Sure, it may seem like he's been gifted more times than Santa's elves on overtime, but I'd like to believe his intentions are wrapped in the shiniest of tinsel. I mean, who wouldn't want to earnestly enrich the lives of their followers and contribute positively to the world, right?

Now, about that dream of his—a tranquil retreat center nestled in the heart of Jamaica. It's a commendable vision, to say the least. A place where people from all walks of life can harmonize with nature and deepen their spiritual practices. Flynn envisions a sanctuary where inner serenity and equilibrium can be found by all who seek it. Oh, and the vision for a rum distillery alongside the yoga huts? Well, that's just his "spiritual" way of creating a sustainable source of income for his community.

At least, that's what I hope he meant.

Santa, if you could muster up some patience and empathy when considering Flynn's requests, I'd be deeply appreciative. Underneath his extra-high self-confidence (or whatever you want to call it) lies a heart brimming with compassion, or so I'd like to believe. Though he may not always convey his intentions with the utmost humility, I'm banking on his genuine desire to make the world a better place.

At least, I'm still hoping so.

In the spirit of unity, compassion, and a dash of irony, I fervently believe that Flynn's aspirations align with the true essence of the holiday season. And if he can find that balance, well, who's to say he won't transform into a modern-day Santa himself?

Time and patience will give us the answer.

As for me, I'm continuing my own journey of reinvention. Last week I tried Zumba. Who knows what might be next!

Thank you, Santa, for dedicating your precious time to read this letter. May your post-holiday season be filled with boundless warmth, love, and profound under-standing (and perhaps a few chuckles).

As always, my hopeful and whimsical regards to both you and Mrs. Claus,

Marilynn Caldwell

FOR IMMEDIATE RELEASE

JAMAICAN SPIRIT GROVE, YOGA RETREAT AND CRAFT RUM DISTILLERY, CELEBRATES A YEAR OF SUCCESSFUL UNITY, SPIRITUAL GROWTH, AND COMMUNITY SUPPORT

[Jamaica] — Spirit Grove, celebrating its one-year anniversary, marks a remarkable year of accomplishment by giving back to both its visitors and the local community. This unique retreat, founded by yoga guru Flynn joined six months ago by business partner Marilynn Caldwell, has exceeded expectations in fostering spiritual growth and leaving guests feeling refreshed relaxed, all while enriching the surrounding community.

Over the past year, Spirit Grove has not only flourished as a sanctuary for spiritual seekers but has also contributed significantly to the local economy. Through the mindful practices and serene environment offered by the retreat, it has generated income for local businesses and provides an economic boost to the people of surrounding towns.

Flynn, renowned for his captivating presence in the world of yoga, acknowledged the invaluable support he received in the past year, which has resulted in the expansion of the Spirit Grove retreat and community.

In the spirit of unity and mindfulness, Flynn, Marilynn Caldwell, and the Spirit Grove community have successfully extended inner peace and serenity to the world during the past year. Surrounded by the natural beauty of Jamaica, this center offers a haven for spiritual growth, meditation, and yoga practice. Spirit Grove provides serene huts nestled in nature, harmonizing with the land's energy to amplify spirituality.

One of the most impressive aspects of Flynn's vision for Spirit Grove is its contribution to the local community. The retreat center, situated amidst the lush Jamaican landscape, has not only amplified spirituality but also become an economic boon for the region. Guests leave the retreat with a sense of inner peace and an eagerness to explore the local businesses and culture, further enriching the community.

Flynn added a rum distillery on the Spirit Grove property. This distillery produces environmentally aware spirits using organic, locally sourced ingredients, enhancing the spiritual experiences of his community while contributing positively to the local economy.

Beloved beauty influencer and social media expert, Nula, recently joined the Spirit Grove team. She brings a unique vision and 3 years of promotional experience. Herbalist Carl will soon be joining the team. He brings with him a lifetime of experience being chill and relaxed and some months of experience growing herbs.

Spirit Grove celebrates its one-year milestone, it invites the world to join in commemorating a year of unity, spiritual growth, relaxation, and community enrichment. For further information or inquiries, please contact:

Media Contact: Nula

Email: nula@jamaicanspiritgrove.com

About Spirit Grove

Spirit Grove is a sacred retreat center nestled amidst the lush hills of Jamaica, dedicated to promoting spiritual growth, mindfulness, and community enrichment through yoga and mindful spirits. Founded by yoga guru Flynn and business partner Marilynn Caldwell, the retreat center has successfully enriched the lives of its visitors while contributing positively to the local economy. With a commitment to sustainability, spirituality, and unity, Spirit Grove aims to create a haven for those seeking inner peace and balance. For more information, contact the newest member of the Spirit Grove team, Nula.

#JamaicanSpiritGrove #MindfulSpirits #SpiritualGrowth

FOR IMMEDIATE RELEASE

SANTA AND MRS. CLAUS EMBARK ON A SPIRITUAL JOURNEY TO JAMAICAN SPIRIT GROVE RETREAT

[Jamaica] — In a heartwarming twist to the holiday season, the world's most beloved couple, Santa and Mrs. Claus, have announced their intention to embark on a well-deserved spiritual journey to the Jamaican Spirit Grove Retreat. From January 1st to January 15th Santa and Mrs. Claus will leave the North Pole behind to rejuvenate their spirits amidst the lush landscape of Jamaica.

Spirit Grove, known for its commitment to mindfulness, spirituality, and community enrichment, is honored to welcome the iconic duo to its tranquil haven. Santa and Mrs. Claus, who have tirelessly spread joy and goodwill throughout the world, have chosen this idyllic retreat for a unique opportunity to unwind and reconnect with their inner selves.

Flynn, the founder of Jamaican Spirit Grove, expressed his enthusiasm for hosting Santa and Mrs. Claus during this special occasion. "We're absolutely stoked to have Santa and Mrs. Claus fly into Spirit Grove! Having them here shows that even the pros in spreading good vibes know it's essential to kick back, recharge, and vibe with the spiritual flow. We're amped up to give them the chillest, most mind-blowing experience ever!" Flynn stated.

This extraordinary visit aligns perfectly with Spirit Grove's mission of offering a sanctuary for those seeking inner peace and balance. Surrounded by the natural beauty of Jamaica, the retreat center offers a unique opportunity for Santa and Mrs. Claus to harmonize with nature, amplify their spirituality, and indulge in mindfulness practices.

Throughout their two-week stay, Santa and Mrs. Claus will have the opportunity to explore the retreat's serene huts, engage in meditation and yoga practices, and immerse themselves in the tranquility of Spirit Grove. Additionally, they will have the privilege of experiencing the center's sustainable and spiritually enriching distillery, which produces mindful spirits using organic, locally sourced ingredients.

The visit of Santa and Mrs. Claus serves as a reminder of the importance of self-care and spiritual growth, even for those who bring happiness to millions. Jamaican Spirit Grove extends a warm welcome to Santa and Mrs. Claus and hopes that their stay will leave them refreshed and ready for another year of spreading joy and goodwill.

For media inquiries or to request interviews during Santa and Mrs. Claus's stay at Jamaican Spirit Grove, please contact:

Media Contact: Nula

Email: nula@jamaicanspiritgrove.com

Note to Social Media Influencers:

If you are a social media influencer

interested in being photographed with Santa and Mrs. Claus during their stay at Jamaican Spirit Grove, contact Nula through the provided email address or phone number. Qualifying influencers may be selected to participate in a social media contest.

About Jamaican Spirit Grove

Jamaican Spirit Grove is a sacred retreat center nestled amidst the lush jungles of Jamaica, dedicated to promoting spiritual growth, mindfullness, and community enrichment through yoga and mindful spirits. Founded by yoga guru Flynn and business partner Marilynn Caldwell, the retreat center has successfully enriched the lives of its visitors while contributing positively to the local economy. With a commitment to sustainability, spirituality, and unity, Jamaican Spirit Grove aims to create a haven for those seeking inner peace and balance. For more information, contact Nula.

**#SantaClaus #MrsClaus
#JamaicanSpiritGrove #SpiritualJourney
#Influencers**

Dear Santa and Mrs. Claus,

Sorry, no time for a letter!
Just this postcard to say thanks for coming all the way down to Spirit Grove for our wedding!
Love,
E & E

Hello again, Gentle Reader,

Thank you for spending part of your holiday with me.
I leave you with my own holiday gratitude—and my personal favorite, county fair award-winning Christmas cookie recipe.

Cheers,
Isabelle Drake

~ ~ ~

Best Ever Recipe for
Cookie Cutter Christmas Cookies

In a medium bowl mix:
3 ¼ cup flour
1 teaspoon baking powder
1 teaspoon baking soda
¼ teaspoon salt

In a large bowl blend together:
1 cup sugar
½ cup shortening
¼ cup room temperature margarine
1 room temperature egg
½ teaspoon vanilla
½ cup milk

- Blend the flour mixture into the sugar mixture.
- Chill for at least 4 hours.
- When you are ready to bake the cookies, preheat the oven to 350 degrees.
- Roll the dough to ¼ inch thick.
- Bake the cookies for 6-8 minutes. Bake longer if the cookies are thicker than ¼ inch.

If you're new to baking cookie cutter cookies, here are some tips:

- Line your baking sheets with parchment paper or silicone baking mats to prevent sticking and make cleanup easier.
- Make sure your oven is fully preheated before baking the cookies.
- Once you add the dry ingredients, mix just until the dough comes together. Overmixing can make cookies tough.
- Generously flour your work surface and rolling pin to prevent dough from sticking.
- Roll the dough to a consistent thickness for even baking.
- After cutting out your shapes, place the cookies on a baking sheet and chill them in the refrigerator for about 15 minutes before baking. This helps them hold their shape.
- For easy decorating, apply sprinkles or colored sugar prior to baking.
- Transfer the baked cookies to a wire rack to cool completely before decorating.
- If you prefer frosting, consider using royal icing for decorating. It dries to a hard, smooth finish and is great for intricate designs.

o Store your decorated cookies in an airtight container to keep them fresh.
o If you need to stack cookies, place parchment paper between layers to prevent sticking or smudging.

Excerpt from
Christmas Spirits

Years ago, in the quaint town of Hickory Hollow, Kentucky, a beautiful girl named Charlotte and a handsome boy named Henry fell in love. Henry's parents insisted he was too young to understand love, while Charlotte's parents urged her to explore other relationships and focus on her education and career before thinking about marriage. In the face of their parents' disapproval, Charlotte and Henry decided to keep their love a secret.

Many moonlit nights, long past midnight, Henry would sneak into Charlotte's family home—a magnificent mansion overlooking the tranquil Ohio River. During the summer, they'd sit in the enchanting garden, sharing stories and laughter. When the chill of winter blanketed the town, Charlotte would clandestinely usher Henry into the mansion, and they would dance and sing in the moonlit ballroom. Together, they dared to dream about their future, a life where their love could flourish.

On December 25th, following Charlotte's 18th birthday celebration dinner, she mustered the courage to confront her parents. She expressed her deep love for Henry and her belief that they were now adults capable of making their own decisions. The two planned to marry after high school graduation. She hoped her parents would understand and grant their blessing, but they did not. Still, her resolve remained unshaken. "You can't control who you fall in love with," she declared. "True love is too precious to cast aside." On that fateful day, Charlotte's parents made a decision that would haunt them, and the entire town of Hickory Hollow, for years to come.

Chapter One

Northern Michigan in November is picturesque. Traverse City is considered one of Michigan's upscale hotspots; it is Hallmark Christmas perfect. It isn't Connecticut, or Maine, I know, but trust me, it is just as photo friendly. The main street that runs through downtown is lined with quaint shops, cafes, and restaurants. There is a retro movie theatre, complete with an old-fashioned marquee circled with blinking lights. A long block away from picturesque downtown is Grand Traverse Bay, part of Lake Michigan. Right now, the water is icy and still. The sandy beach is dotted with piles of snow, rounded mounds coated with a glitter frosting of ice. Later, in February, the bay will come alive again. Hand-built fishing shanties will pop up across the bay. But for now, there is only the snow, ice, and fluffy white clouds floating above, making the sky look as though Santa and his reindeer had just flown by.

Tourists, wrapped in brightly colored scarves, heads topped with knit pompom caps, stroll up and down the walk that runs the length of the bay before turning to loop back into town for some shopping and refreshments. Hot chocolate topped with whipped cream, dry martinis dotted with olives, hand-crafted pizza, fudge of all flavors—with and without nuts, sushi… visitors can find all and more that as they work their way through the streets, gazing into the holiday themed store fronts and strolling beneath the strings of twinkling lights.

It's the end of the third week of November, a Saturday morning, and I'm inside my bakery, Northern Lights Cakes & Café. None of the tourists pop in for a blueberry muffin or a loaf of my award-winning pumpkin bread. A few pause at the wide window and peer in. Some of them spot me inside and wave. The ones who do reach for the door, see the colorful sign I'd posted right above the lock late last Wednesday night: *Thank you for the good times. I'm closed for business.* Below the tidy printing are the handwritten words I added yesterday afternoon after several of my regulars tried to yell at me through the glass. *The building has been sold. Thanks for being such great customers.* Even though I didn't feel in the mood to, I'd picked up a red marker and drawn a big smiley face in the lower right corner. For an extra touch I'd added a jaunty Santa hat. That festive addition seemed to make people laugh, so now when our gazes connected, they smiled and most of the time I managed to smile in return.

Inside, I'm wrapping up the last box of decorated sugar cookies I'll ever deliver. On the sidewalk outside, a couple is making their way down the sidewalk, pushing a stroller with a drowsy puppy tucked into the small basket tied between the handles. A baby sleeps below. My brother Johan appears beside them and starts scratching the chocolate lab pup's head. Flurries settle across his shoulders, quickly melting into the red and black plaid wool of his coat. Some land on his beard. Those stay, looking like crumbs. He points across the street as the couple, now laughing, head toward the corner.

I unlatch the door, he slips inside, bringing a draft of cold air and a few snowflakes with him. I relock the door and greet him without the false cheer I've been offering everyone else. He grabs me into a bear hug, holding me against his cold, snowy chest. I stay there, leaning on him just like I have been ever since I've been strong enough to stand.

"Going okay, I see." He's speaking over the top of my head, his voice soft and solemn. "Want me to carry those taped-up boxes to the van?"

I swallow the lump in my throat, then ease away from his chest. There is no hiding my sad sniffles, so I don't bother trying. "Keys are on the hook."

After he grabs the keys and two of the boxes, the bells on the back door jungle as he exits out the back. I step over to the front corner window that faces the sidewalk and start pulling the games and puzzles off the cluttered low shelves. Across the street on the opposite corner, the woman who owns the bookstore is decorating the fir tree that grows outside the door to her shop. Some of the locals are with her, holding the ladder for each other as they take turns placing the ornaments on the high branches. A couple of German Shepards are chasing each other, bouncing against a pair of toddler twins holding their mom's hands.

With a sigh, I go back to tearing apart the cozy atmosphere I'd spent the past three years building. Season after season, I'd updated the games, look-books, and toys. I'd swapped out the throw blankets the couples liked to cozy up with for woven floor mats kids used to sit on the floor in the busy, warmer months. Now, it was all getting broken down and tossed into boxes. With no plans to unpack anything anytime soon, I simply grab whatever is within reach and twist back to plop it into one of the boxes. Thanks to my unenthusiastic, haphazard method, one of the puzzle tops pops off and the box tips sideways. The box sways above the floor then all 350 oversize pieces tumble onto the floor.

I sit back on my heels, looking at the pile, unable to stop the sniffles from turning into full fledge tears. Johan finds me that way, crying as I point to the pile of pieces.

"Look, it's my life in abstract." Yet again, I put on a fake smile.

He presses a wad of napkins into my palm, then drops to the floor to start scooping up the pieces. I blow my nose then set the bottom of the box between us.

"I'm sorry Paisley." The pieces make a light thump as he drops them into the box. "This sucks. Not just for you, but for…" he waves to the street, "everyone."

"Thanks." I'm done sniffling. I do the childish thing of tossing the used napkins across the room. What difference does it make? I'll be the one who picks them up later.

He continues scooping the pieces and dropping them into the box. Once the mess is cleared, I pick up the top. He takes it from me, pausing right before slipping it over the lower tray. He flips it all the way over, staring at something written on the underside of the top.

He sets the lid on the floor and points to the note printed across the middle. "You should do it."

"Call her?"

He taps on the message. "Yeah."

"People don't mean that sort of thing." He's nodding. I'm shaking my head. "It's just something they say to be nice. Like, *let's get lunch sometime*."

He taps again. "She meant it."

I remember the afternoon she'd spent curled up in the biggest overstuffed chair, reading a romance novel and occasionally offering cake decorating tips we both knew I didn't need. That had been two and a half years ago, but the warm emotions of the day were still deep inside me. Maybe she did mean what she'd written. I flip the lid over and slide it onto the box. "I can't afford the gas money to get all the way down to Kentucky."

"How—" Johan's insistence is cut short by the rattle of keys in the door. It's Ronny Randall from Randall's Realty ignoring the fact that I still have possession through the weekend and bustling his way into the shop. He doesn't bother locking the door behind himself, so I get up to hit the latch.

"How's it going Paisley? Need help with anything?" Without waiting for a reply, he steps further in, puts his hands on his hips and pivots to assess my progress. His gaze combs across the bare shelves, stacks of boxes, then zeroes in on the lone box on the counter. "Are you still doing business?"

"No." I gesture to the half-packed boxes and general chaos but he's still staring at the box. "That's a donation."

He lumbers over to examine the bright yellow box wrapped with fat rust and gold striped ribbon.

Afraid he's going to touch it, I add, "It's a *gift*."

He pivots again, "Are you still baking things? Here? Because I—"

"I'm helping her pack." Johan stands up and comes to my side.

I set my hand on his forearm. "I'll be out of here by tomorrow night. That's our agreement."

"Yeah. It was. The thing is, it's going to be busy later this week, with Thanksgiving coming, and…"

… all those paying customers wanting baked goods for the holiday.

151

"My wife wants to have a soft opening, um, tomorrow night."

Johan stiffens. My stomach knots.

"She wants to invite some friends and family in, to, um, see her new space. You know what I mean?"

I do know what he means because I'd done the same thing after I redesigned this space to be a bakery cafe. The same space Ms. Randall was about to drop herself into.

"Think you can be out by noon tomorrow instead? Or maybe even 11:30?"

Still holding my brother's arm, my shoulder hits the door when I take a step back.

"And, well, she isn't going to have time to bake anything, so, she's um, wondering if you could, well, make her a cake?"

Is this terribly funny or terribly terrible? Should I laugh or cry?

I don't get a chance to decide because he rushes in with, "She'll pay you more than your usual price, for the, um, rush order and all."

Rush orders are expensive. "I can make a sheet cake, half size." To his blank stare, I add, "That's about 58 servings."

"Oh sure." The keys jangle as he flips his palms through the space in front of him. "That'd be fine."

"And it'll be decorated with whatever I have on hand." I let go of Johan's sleeve, fold my arms across my chest, then offer him a price four times my usual overnight rush rate.

* * *

Hours later, long after Johan left, the chime of the cheery bells attached to the back exit fades as the door swings shut. My turn to leave this time. The flurries have gotten fatter, the clouds thicker, and the sun much lower. The festive box is now wrapped with clear cellophane, so the occasional snowflakes leave shining droplets as they melt. The setting sun and stormy weather make the lights from the shop windows and restaurant fronts cozier and more inviting. Downtown will be busy for several more hours, but where I'm headed won't be packed with tourists. I cut through the far corner of downtown, my boots sinking into the wet snow as my pace quickens.

I turn onto a side street, and the neighborhood is as quiet as I expect. Victorian homes with delicate gingerbread trim line both sides of the street. When I reach the tiniest, narrowest one of the block, I slow down and glance over my shoulder. Aside from mine, there are no footprints on the sidewalk. The little walkway that leads to the narrow pink door is still covered with snow. There are no lights on and no sign of movement. I glance around again, to make sure I am alone and unseen, and hurry to the front porch. Gently I go up the steps. Once on the porch, I set the box on the welcome mat and pat the pretty bow with my palm.

Goodbye.

Keeping my steps light, I backtrack through my own footprints. I take a few steps then pause on the sidewalk to take a final look up and down the street. I'd walked through this neighborhood dozens of times, but this is the first time I'd come up to the house.

"Hey lady."

A boy comes down the steps of the house next door. He runs into the center of the yard. "You looking for Ms. Emaline?" he yells after picking up a stuffed bear covered with snow.

I hurry closer to him and answer with a soft voice. "I just have a delivery for the house."

"Do you know Ms. Emaline?"

I glance at the tiny pink house, quiet and dark, then look back to the boy. Not trusting my voice as I turn back to him, I shake my head.

His eyebrows drop. "Then why are you bringing her cookies?"

"I—she—those are samples. I want to see if she likes them."

"Oh. I bet she will. I mean would. I think she left." He points to the driveway I'd just crossed over. "There was a truck there the other day. One of the big kinds with the giant doors on the back."

"A moving truck?"

"I can't read yet."

"Did it look like they were filling the truck with furniture?"

"Like couches and chairs and stuff like that?"

I nod.

He nods.

Gone. Again.

"I tell you what. If the box is still there tomorrow at lunch time, you can go over and take it." I spot his mom watching him from their window. "Ask your mom, though. Okay?"

"What kind of samples are in the box?"

"Cookies shaped like turkeys."

"Do they have sprinkles? Frosting?"

"Yes. And yes." I wave at his mom, and she waves back.

"Yum!" He smacks the bear against his leg and snow flies upward into his face. "I can share them with B Bear."

"Ask your mom, though, before you go over and take the box. Okay?"

Backing away, he nods again.

His mom and I exchange waves again then I force myself to walk away.

On the night Charlotte told her parents of her plans to share her life with Henry, they informed their daughter that if she chose to marry him, they would not attend the wedding. It was a painful ultimatum that shattered Charlotte's heart. How could she reconcile her love for Henry with her love for her parents? The start of her new year was filled with misery and confusion, yet their love and longing to build a life together grew.

Days after high school graduation, their love story took an unexpected turn. The world changed and the pair of lovers understood that their needs weren't the only needs that mattered. Henry, enlisted in the military. He promised Charlotte he would return to her. She assured him that she understood his need to serve and that she would wait for him. So, with his heart filled with hope for their future together, he left their quaint and cozy Kentucky town. Charlotte awaited Henry's return. News of the war reached Hickory Hollow, and the town was filled with stories of bravery and sacrifice. Months turned into years, and Henry never came back.

Chapter Two

"No, it'll never work." Lucas Lee backed away from his brother and the bright red bag he had clutched in his arms. "I'm not big enough or old enough to be your Santa."

"The beard will cover most of your face, and we have this." Lucas' brother, Mason, upended the bag and shook out the contents. He dug through to find a wad of white stuffing, the kind their mom used to fill her needlepoint pillows. "Once you're in the suit, we'll just cram a bunch of this in there. You'll be fat and jolly in no time." The pile of bright red velvet his brother had dumped onto the bland couch of his bland month-to-month rented condo spilled over onto the bland beige carpet floor. Mason tried to use his I'm your older brother, so I know what's best stare, as he added, "You did say you wanted to reconnect with the community."

Those had been Lucas' exact words. And he did want to do that but was dressing up as a fat old man really the only way to accomplish that objective? "Don't *you* want to do it?" he asked. "After all, you're the one with kids."

"That is exactly why I can't do it. You're not in LA anymore. This is Hickory Hollow. All the kids know me. And they all know all the other dads in town. Nobody knows you, so you are the perfect man for the job." Still holding the wad of stuffing, he grabbed the pants and tossed them toward Lucas. "Go ahead. Try them on."

"Fine, fine. I'll try them on but that doesn't mean I am agreeing to any of this." Keeping his grey joggers on, he stepped into the oversized pants. Holding the waistband all the way out, looked down into the gap that wasn't quite as big as he'd expected and added, "You sure you have this much stuffing?"

"If we don't have enough, I'll just get some more." Mason tossed the jacket and Lucas caught it with his free hand.

Mason's wife, Jill, replied as she sauntered into the room. "Once we start telling everyone you, the town's newest bachelor, will be the Santa…"

Lucas stopped snapping and passed a mock glare from Jill to Mason.

"Don't look like that," she said. "This is a fund-raising event. Be nice."

When he looked up, he caught the tight-lipped expressions on both Lucas and Jill. His sister and law caught his eye and covered her mouth. "I'm glad the two of you are so entertained." With a half-smiled of his own, he returned to the task of snapping up the suit jacket. "Since it's a fundraiser, can't I just offer some funds instead and hire someone else to be Santa?"

He finished the snaps, grabbed the waistband of the pants and went to the mirror hanging in the hall. "I'm trying to be serious," he said. Between bursts of his own laughter, he added, "That was a serious question."

Mason was bent over now, barely managing to stand. Jill was leaning on him, her body shaking as she wiped tears from her cheeks. Lucas had to admit, he was a hilarious sight. All those years of honing his image as the consummate professional, the ultra-capable renovator of the rich and famous, now looking like a deflated mall Santa.

As much as he hated to admit it, his brother was right, the guy did have a point. He'd come back to Kentucky to stay. He'd done what he set out to accomplish and honestly it had left him feeling as deflated as the Santa suit. So, he'd done the whole big business thing and now wanted to like and know the people he worked with and who worked for him. Sure, he'd still travel for jobs and events, but aside from his carer disappointments, his nieces and nephews were growing up so fast. If he didn't make time to spend with them, he was going to miss out.

Priorities, he reminded himself. "Alright, alright. Stop laughing. I'll be your Santa." He smoothed down the white faux fur trim running down his front. "There is one condition."

Mason dropped himself on to the couch and picked up another piece of the stuffing. "An endless supply of cookies?"

Jill sat down next to him. "Extra marshmallows in your hot chocolate?"

"Ha, ha. Very funny." Lucas shuffled over to grab the wad of stuffing from his brother but stopped short. He lifted up a remaining pile of faux fur trimmed with red velvet. "Wait—what is this?"

Jill grinned. "That will be for Mrs. Claus, of course."

* * *

About 12 hours after I'd left the shop, Johan and I returned. He'd boxed up the rest of small things, like the table lamps and boxes of wood carved coasters that the kids played with, but the customers never used, and the collection of dogs toys I kept by the front door, then he'd hauled out the chairs. The collection of small tables he'd made over the years from the lake driftwood he collected while doing his fishing charters were scattered around the shop reminding me of unruly toy soldiers.

As he came and went, I continued packing the kitchen. Measured tools, flour scoops, seasonal sugar toppings, it all went in the boxes. All except the few decorating items I'd selected and left out. The whole time I worked, the bare half sheet cake, now out of the pan, sat on the cooling rack. Johan hadn't said anything about that last task and neither had I. The only sound between us had been the jingle of the bells hung over the back door. Still, his presence reassured me that somehow, I'd get the frosting on the cake and then get myself out the door on time. What was going to happen after that, I had no idea.

Right after I drop in the last of my spatulas, he comes in holding the bells aloft.

"Take them?" He shakes the strand, the familiar sound bittersweet. "Leave them?"

"Leave them." I reply over my shoulder as I move to stand in front of the cake.

The bells jangle as he hangs them back up. Back in the front room, he says, "I'm going to take the van home. I'll come back for you in my Jeep." He picks up the long knife I use for trimming the edges then comes over. "How long… what time do you want me to come back?"

I take it from him then start on the first side. "A couple minutes after 12:00."

"They might be here sooner." He picks up the discarded strip of cake, folds it in half and takes a bite even though its still cool from the freezer. After a swallow, he says, "Pumpkin spice?"

"Yep."

He smiles, brushing crumbs out of his beard. "You hate pumpkin spice in cakes."

"Yeah. But everyone else loves it. And the cake isn't for me." I start on the next side, my hands seeming to do the work against my mind's will. "I know he said they might get here at 11:30, but I don't want you stuck standing around."

"Why don't you have them send you the payment? That way you don't have to be here to see…"

I take a look around the empty space. Soon, it'll be filled with strangers and soon after that it will no longer be mine. "She's going to pay me in cash."

"I'll come early, so you don't have to be here by yourself." He finishes the rest of the piece of cake in two bites. Tiny bits of golden cake fall onto the counter. "Because it's not being stuck; it's called being supportive." He picks up another discarded side piece of cake and again folds it in half.

I brush away his crumbs then trim the second and third edges, setting the long strips near where he stands. "You've been listening to too many self-help podcasts."

"Are you complaining?"

"Nope." I glance at him with a half-smile. A real one this time. "Just looking for the chance to harass you."

He scoops up the other two edge strips, one on top of the other, and stacks them on top of each other then folds them half together. When we were little kids *helping* our mom make cakes, we called them cake sandwiches.

"I'll be back at 11:25," he says, then opens wide.

My smile lingers a little longer but is gone again by the time the bells stop ringing. To fill in the silence I flip on my favorite track of coffee house jazz and then continue prepping the cake by laying the cardboard serving tray across the top. After I slide the cake back into the freezer, I start on the cream cheese frosting.

Soon enough the mixer is humming, and the motions of my work have relaxed me. I'm so relaxed that when I hear the tapping on the door, I look up and smile. It's a real smile, but it freezes on my mouth when I realize who is on the other side of the door.

She waves.

I go to the door, and even though I want to yank the door open, I point at the sign.

She's nodding and speaking, but the whirr of the mixer drowns out her words. I unlatch the door and open it a crack then back away to shut off the mixer. When I turn back around, she's stepped in the room and is standing just inside the doorway, holding the door in one hand and waving awkwardly with the other.

"Leo's mom told me about the samples. That you left them on my doorway. I just had to say thank you."

"Oh, sure." I lifted my hand, mimicking her awkward gesture. Why hadn't it occurred to me that the little boy's mom might know *her*?

"I heard about the shop closing, so I figured you… you… were leaving the samples because you are moving to a new place."

Said aloud, it made no sense, of course. So, we stand there, staring into each other's deep chocolate brown eyes making similar tongue-tied expressions with our look alike bow-shaped mouths.

"Where will your new shop be?"

The coffee house jazz fills our silence for several long seconds until finally I figure out something to say. "I—I—don't have plans. No yet." All the things I want to

162

tell her and to ask her stay inside me, churning with the all too familiar long buried pain and confusion. "The little boy next door said you're moving."

"Leo. It's been fun watching him grow up." Still holding on to the edge of the door, she leans against the jam. The bend of her neck reveals an intricate ivy tattoo that is partly embedded in her hair and then runs down the side of her neck. "Yes, I guess I am. Moving."

Watching him grow up.

"Did you sell the house?" It would be a really inappropriate question to ask a stranger, but we both know we aren't strangers. But what we are now, today, hasn't been defined. It hasn't even been discussed. Or said aloud.

"No. I didn't sell it."

I shrug. "I bet Ronny Randall would be happy to list it for you."

She laughs, but it's a dry chuckle from the back of her throat and ends with a soft cough.

"I'm sorry about what they did with your shop," she says, now swinging the door back in forth. A few dry leaves are pulled inside from the motion. "What they are doing, going to do." She gazes around at the empty space, her attention landing on the stuff laid out for the cake. "So, you're moving too."

"Guess so."

She taps one of the leaves with the toe of her worn black Dr. Marten's. "Where to?"

It's only now, hearing her ask the question, that I realize I am moving. I have to move. My life here is gone and I don't have the heart—or money—to rebuild. There is one possibility, but instead of saying it, I swallow hard and shrug. "Don't know," I say. "What about you?

where—" My question faulters as a woman ducks under my mom's arm and slips inside.

She's grinning and gazing around, completely unaware that she's broken up the one conversation I've ever had with my biological mother. If there was a chance to ask, to tell, to talk, its gone now as Ronny Randall's wife marches across the floor, swinging her arms as though she owns the place because, in fact, she does.

In the aftermath of Henry's disappearance, Charlotte's emotions remained a mystery to everyone. She never spoke of her plans for the future, and she never told anyone of a plan to leave her hometown to seek out her lost love. One night while the moon was high, she gathered a few of her belongings and climbed out her window. And so, both she and Henry seemed to have vanished without a trace, leaving behind only questions and rumors. Some believed Henry had met a heroic end on the battlefield, and Charlotte was too heartbroken to return home. Others insisted that he had found a way to return to her, and they were living happily in secret.

Their mysterious story united the two families in grief and remorse. Beliving their children had truly vanished from the world, the parents set a single tombstone on the hillside cemetery behind the mansion. The spot, with its gentle slope leading down to the river, was where the lovers had often daydreamed about their future escape.

Legend has it that Charlotte and Henrey, two star-crossed spirits, remain bound to the mansion, tethered by an unfinished love story. Only one event will free them from their eternal attachment—another couple must take their place. Two must meet and fall in love within the mansion's walls. To this day, the mansion stands as a lonely sentinel, and the townsfolk of Hickory Hollow avoid it, knowing that the ghosts of Charlotte and Henry still roam its halls, searching, waiting, and yearning for the day when they can finally play matchmaker and set themselves free.

About the Author

Isabelle Drake is the fiction alias of Melissa Ford Lucken. She holds an MFA in Creative Writing from Lasell University and an MA in Special Education from Eastern Michigan University. She teaches creative writing and composition and is the editor of the *Washington Square Review*.

Find Isabelle Drake on Amazon, Facebook, YouTube, BookBub, Goodreads, Instagram, X, and all the other socials. Find Melissa Ford Lucken on Amazon, Instagram, X, Goodreads, and Facebook.

If You Like This Title, You Might Also Like

Everglades Wildfire
By Isabelle Drake

Satisfaction Guaranteed
By Isabelle Drake

Mistress of the Undead
By Isabelle Drake

Servant of the Undead
By Isabelle Drake

Disciple of the Undead
By Isabelle Drake

The Binge Watcher's Guide to Riverdale
By Melissa Ford Lucken

www.ingramcontent.com/pod-product-compliance
Lightning Source LLC
Chambersburg PA
CBHW050658290626
47170CB00015B/1685